CW01521645

# Mandorlinfiore

## And Other Italian Folk Tales

Simon Kellow Bingham

Published in 2020 by Simon Kellow-Bingham.

First Edition.

Copyright © Text Simon Kellow-Bingham
.

The author asserts the moral right under the Copyright, Designs and Patents Act 1988 to be identified as the author of this work.

All Rights Reserved. No part of this publication may be reproduced, stored in a retrieval system, or transmitted, in any form or by any means without prior written consent of the author, nor be otherwise circulated in any form of binding or cover other than that in which it is published and without a similar condition being imposed on the subsequent purchaser.

Published by Simon Kellow-Bingham.
All Rights reserved. 2020.

ISBN- 9798635877449

Copyright © Photography Simon Kellow-Bingham
Copyright © Dragon Illustration Maya Kellow-Bingham
Copyright © Bandit Illustrations Jemima Kellow-Bingham

# Contents

*Mappe of Southern Corsica.*

# Mandorlinfiore

# 1. A Ship Arrives

There is a port on the South Eastern shore of the island of Corsica that is ideal for trade from mainland Italy, from Sardinia, Spain and Africa. It is easy to defend from pirates and other seafaring brigands and so it has prospered. Our story begins many years ago, before there were steam trains or flying machines, when the world was perhaps a simpler place, though not without its difficulties.

A grand trading ship has just docked in the port this evening and the passengers are alighting. See there? That man is the King of Zonza. He has been away to see someone in Marseille on some political business and by the look of his pallor he is happy to be back on dry land. Over there is a grand merchant from Solenzara unloading his wares from the ship and stacking them onto his wagons.

The King looks ready to hurry back to his castle in the mountains. It is said that his fiancé is waiting for him. Indeed, had we been here just two days ago we would have seen a ship under the Royal flag of Spain on this very water.

The King's men assemble and ready the horses and then they are off, at a sedate pace along the quay. The merchant looks set to be off by sunrise. Only the King dares travel the island's roads by night. It is said that there is sorcerer's blood in him and that there is no night creature you care to think of that can make him afraid. But do not misunderstand me; the King is still a man after all.

Now the merchant and the King both have a role to play in our story. At this moment neither is aware of their part in it, nor may they ever meet again, or be in such close quarters as they once were aboard ship. Everything we do, every action we make, or decision we take will add up over time and bring us to where we are. We are a collection of our decisions, good and bad. We can't help it; it's the way we move through life, choosing left, or right, up, or down.

## 2. A Baby is Born

I suppose that now is probably the best time to really start telling the story.

Once upon a time, that's how all the best stories start. Am I right? Well, let's see. Once upon this time there was a husband and a wife, soon to become a father and a mother. He was a fisherman, keen eyed and hardy; she was a seamstress, quick with a needle and thread. Now they might have been poor, but they were moderately happy, in good health, with some fine friends. They didn't want for much more than to have a family, and so it was with great joy that they discovered that the wife was to have their first child.

Our story starts on the fateful night that sets the future for all of us, the night of the baby's birth. In this town it was the custom for the husband to stand at the door, ready to announce to the community the name and status of the new arrival. Our young husband had been on tenterhooks all day long. He longed for a son he could take to sea, as he had been taken to sea by his father before him. In this town it was also the belief that whoever might be passing the front door at the moment of the child's birth would bestow their particular fate upon the baby. To counter this it was usual for the family's friends to guard the door so that no undesirable persons may come anywhere near.

On the night in question however, we find that the tides have not been kind and all of the husband's associates are out at sea, and all of their wives are otherwise engaged either with the new mother or with their own babies.

And so it was that a small gang of pirates, deep in their cups and singing bawdy songs, clattering their cutlass and spurs, came staggering along the quay. And the husband called out to his wife; 'For goodness sake, don't have the baby just yet.'

She did not have the baby then and the husband was relieved. But when he looked up again he saw a pair of slavers with their cruel whips tied at their belts. And the husband called out to his wife, 'not yet, not yet.'

She did not have the baby then and the husband was relieved. But when he looked up again, he saw a madam and her girls trotting down to the quay. And the husband called out to his wife, 'please, not yet.'

She did not have the baby then and the husband was relieved. He prayed for his friends to return safely with the tide to protect the fate of his family. But when he looked up again who should he see outside his door but the King, and right at that very moment a son was born to his wife. At once the new father cried out; 'A King has been born to us! A King has been born to us.' And there was much rejoicing within the house.

3. Of Kings and Fishermen

Now the King himself was not much abroad at this time of night in this particular town, nor was he used to the ways of this place, however, he was a very superstitious man. He had come by the crown through the wiles of a Mazerre, a Corsican shapeshifter who had found him in the mountains, lost and orphaned, many years ago. On hearing the fisherman's proclamation that a King had been born he ordered that his men announce him at the door.

'His Highness the King of Zonza!' they proclaimed, for it was he.

The new father had at once gone into the house to see the new baby boy and appeared at the door with him in his arms.

'He's very small for a King,' remarked the King of Zonza, for at that time he was still quite young and was not familiar with children, 'Still, since I am a King and you are a poor fisherman it should make much more sense that you should surrender the child to me such that I may school him in the ways of Kings. I have no children of my own after all.'

'I am sorry my King, but I cannot give up our son to you. To be a fisherman is to be a King of the seas. This boy will command a boat, not a Kingdom. He will be master of nets, not of men.'

The King of Zonza considered the fisherman's case and he wondered whether he was being hasty, but as he surveyed the poor fisherman's lowly cottage and remembered the rough sea crossing, he had made from Italy the year before, his resolve became firm.

'You will give the child to me. He will be schooled in the talents required for Kingship. He will eat well and be dressed well and be accepted into the finest courts in Europe.'

'But your Highness I cannot give up our only child,' cried the father. His wife called out in alarm and the women filled the tiny room at the front of the cottage.

'You will have more children; just make sure you have no more Kings.'

'I cannot allow it sir,' said the father,

Outraged at being denied his will the King ordered that the child be taken from the father by force if necessary. At once the King's men had the points of their swords at the father's throat and stomach. One blade slid behind his neck.

'You will give me the child, or I will have both the child and your head fisherman,' said the King, 'ask your wife what to do for the best.'

Seeing her husband caught up in so much royal steel scared his wife to the point of complete despair, 'Spare my husband and spare my baby boy. You might take him and make him a King, but he will always be a fisherman in his heart.'

And so, the King of Zonza was able to take the newly born King from the arms of his father and bear him up onto his horse. The King's men fell back and let the fisherman sink to his knees. The last the new mother saw that night was her child borne away upon the road that led into the mountains.

### 4. The King's Dilemma

It may be true that the King of Zonza was schooled in the ways of Kingship, but his knowledge of children was slight and so, by sunrise, he had tired of the infant's constant mewling. In his mind the noise the child made was far from royal and he began to doubt his contention that to raise a stranger's child to be his heir was the right thing to do. In the light of day, it all seemed a terribly rash thing to have done, after all, the fisherman had seemed a decent sort. But then he couldn't undo what he had done and return the child, as that would mean having to admit that he had made a bad decision. It was a puzzle indeed.

If he was to return the child, then fate might just raise him up to be a challenger to the crown of Zonza. If he were to keep the child, then he might grow up to betray him and so also win the crown of Zonza. The only thing he could do would be to kill the child for then it would be beyond the reach of Gods and men.

At that moment the King saw that he had come to a small almond grove. He ordered his men to guard his horse and went through the gate. And so he took the infant and placed him between the roots of an almond tree. The King of Zonza then drew his sword and placed the tip upon the baby's throat. As the blade dug into the soft skin of the newborn and the bright red petals of first blood welled onto the royal steel the King shuddered. Although he had no skill or knowledge of children, he found himself repelled by his own action and so he withdrew the blade.

It happened that the grove was also home to the local breed of hardy mountain pig. They were friendly, curious creatures, but they had the reputation that they would eat anything left on the ground.

'May the pigs eat you or keep you. If fate determines then I will wait to put you to the sword when you are a man.'

With that the King of Zonza wiped the stain from his blade on the grass at the foot of the almond tree and climbed back upon his horse. On his return to the citadel of Zonza he found a Princess, a daughter of the King of Spain and her ladies in waiting. The King was due to marry the Princess, which he did. He fell in love with her in good time and they had a beautiful daughter between them whom they called Belfioré. The King of Zonza, by and by, forgot about the fisherman's son completely.

*The wild interior of Corsica.*

## 5. The Merchant's Discovery

As has been said before, the pigs of this region are a tough, but curious and friendly breed. They spend their days foraging on the woodland floor for fungi, fallen fruit and nuts, and their nights curled up together under rocky outcrops or in ruined swineherd's huts. In those days wolves and other wild beasts roamed the interior and a mountain pig was a feast.

The pigs that had made their home in this almond grove were as friendly and curious as any other and so, when they heard the cries of the baby boy, they were quickly snuffling and snorting about him. He was about the size

14

and colour of a large piglet and still retained some aroma of his mother's milk.

By some miracle of nature, a young sow who had already weaned three litters, took a liking to the child and suckled him for a night and a day.

Now it happened that the King had been followed up the mountain the next day by the merchant from Solenzara, with whom he had crossed the Tyrhennian Sea. The merchant dealt in fine cloth from the East and rare herbs from the North, jewels from the South and gold from the West.

He and his wife had been faithful servants of the Lord and their King and had once had hope that one day they too would be blessed with children. Alas the merchant and his wife had begun to think they would never have a child to call their own.

And so the merchant was in a low mood as his horse and wagon toiled up the rocky path into the interior. By the time he reached the almond grove it was near midday.

From here there was a fine view across the valley down to the sea and the almond trees were in full flower. The merchant thought it a proper place to rest his horse in the shade.

He climbed down from the wagon and tied his horse and then stepped into the grove to rest his back against a tree. As he sat, he noticed a small bundle of rags between the roots.

He made to pick them over when he heard a small cry from within the bundle. Gently he raised up the rags and discovered the baby within. His heart leapt.

'Praise God,' he said, and then looked all about for the child's parents. All he saw were pigs. He called out, appealing for the child's parents to come forward. 'Surely there can be no-one able to leave such a tiny creature all alone with these wild pigs?'

He looked more closely at the child and spied the wound on his neck. The merchant knew then that the baby had no other opportunity than to go with him, to be raised as his own. He looked up to the sky and could see only almond blossom.

'Lord, I name this child Cut-Neck.'

## 6. Almond-Blossom

The merchant took up the boy and bore him home to his wife. She was agog at the story her husband had to tell and gave thanks to the Lord for the gift of a baby at last.

'But Cut-Neck is the name for a brigand or a pirate,' said his wife, 'and I should never want to call such a man my son.'

'But his neck?' said the merchant,

'Silly man,' said his wife, 'you said you found the boy in an almond grove with swine?'

'I'll not call him Pig-Boy,'

'Indeed not,'

'Then what?'

'He must be called Mandorlinfiore, for the Almond-Blossom, to match the light in his eyes.'

'Wife, you are a romantic indeed. It is a handsome name. Let us tell the priest and gather our families for the christening!'

Now this act of charity was swiftly rewarded by the angels and not more than a year later the merchant and his wife had a son between them whom they called Mandorlinfiore, and the merchant of Solenzara, by the grace of God, grew richer every day.

Mandorlinfiore and Sylvan were great friends as children and played from dawn to dusk. As they grew older however, the differences between them became more marked. While Mandorlinfiore was keen to put to sea with the traders, Sylvan was preoccupied with keeping shop. Mandorlinfiore grew to be a tall, slender young man with a shock of fine black hair and far seeing dark brown eyes, while Sylvan was stocky, with a back as strong as any ox. Nevertheless, both were excellent bookkeepers and their father and mother were proud of both of them.

One day, when Mandorlinfiore was a young man the merchant and his wife sat down with him to tell him the story of how he came to be their son. Now you would think that such a miracle might have gladdened the heart of anyone, but at once a cloud entered the eyes of Mandorlinfiore and he at once vowed revenge on whoever had abandoned him.

The merchant and his wife tried to explain that it would be an impossible vow to keep as there was no clue as to his original heritage.

'It is as likely that you are the son of a mountain swineherd lost in a crevasse, as that you are the son of the Chamberlain of Zonza,' they reasoned, 'the rags we found you wrapped in were burned a long time ago.'

'But it was an evil deed!'

'That may be so my son,' said his mother, 'but it was our miracle that the angels delivered you to us.'

'And Sylvan? Was he discovered in a basket on the shore?'

'No.'

'That is his good fortune and I am happy for him, but I must seek out my fate.' said Mandorlinfiore, 'I will leave in the morning and discover God's will.'

And so he set out the very next morning on his father's second-best horse and with a small purse of gold.

'May God bring you home to us safe and sound,' said his mother as she watched her child borne away upon the road that led into the mountains.

## 7. The King's Daughter

Now all this time had passed and what had become of the King of Zonza, his consort and his daughter. Well the King was troubled by the poor accounting of his men and was every day worried that his fortune should be lost from under his nose. He sought every day the wisdom of an old Mazerre, who by now was so old he had been turned to stone. His wife, once a daughter of the King of Spain and now the Queen of Zonza, was usually bored with the meagre court life that there was on offer in the mountainous Kingdom of Zonza and was often abroad with her cousins in Rome or other such places.

She was unable to persuade her headstrong daughter, the beautiful Princess Belfioré, to accompany her on such trips and so the girl was left to her own amusements. These included the twin sports of falconry and archery. Her mother had many times tried to distract Belfioré with needlecrafts and the pianoforte but to no avail. Belfioré had brought her falcon to piano lessons and decorated a quiver in needlecraft.

By the time she was eighteen Belfioré was an assured fencer, horsewoman and huntress. Her mother was exasperated while her father was proud.

'We must find her a husband,' the Queen of Zonza would say to the King.

'What for?' he would say, 'She will make a fine Queen one day. Anyway, I am sure Belfioré is more than capable of finding her own husband.'

In point of fact Princess Belfioré had little time for either the Princes, or the Lords, or even the many Knights that would visit the mountain Kingdom from time to time. The Princes seemed all too vain, the Lords too high and mighty, and the Knights too full of machismo, in desperate need of a damsel. They would all be sent packing by Belfioré, and most would go north to Ajaccio and sail back to the mainland.

It is said that one such wandering Knight, heading higher into the mountains to the Kingdom of Corté, escaped from the mountain wolves to be captured by a race of giants, but that is another story. In fact, the mountains of Zonza had their own reputation for treacherous inhabitants, ready to way-lay the traveller and hunter alike. The peculiar character of the area attracted adventurers and fortune seekers, who oftentimes never returned. The reality was that many of them would find pleasant employment in Zonza, where they would remain, fearful of making the return journey through such terrible places. But for Princess Belfioré, who had grown up knowing no other place than the precipitous slopes of Zonza's forests, the yawning bottomless chasms into which its rivers fell, and the icy points of its mountains, there was no such terror. She had set out on her horse as often as she could from the age of eight to discover the limits of her father's realm. She knew where the giants took their water, where the wolves would wait in ambush, where the Mazerre would gather to tell their stories and what had happened to the wandering Knight.

And then, one fateful day, she saw Mandorlinfiore on the mountain road through the Forest of Zonza, and she fell in love.

## 8. A Magical Discovery

Mandorlinfiore was not a skilled horseman, nor a hunter, but he was always able to coax fish from water, be it sea or stream, and this is how he had been able to sustain himself on his quest to avenge his abandonment. On his first day in the mountains there was bread in his bag freshly baked in Solenzara. On his second day he had nothing but fish to eat. On his third day he met an adventurer, set on capturing a giant, with whom he was able to trade his fish for some cake.

It was on this third day in the mountains that Mandorlinfiore came upon an almond grove. Behind its low walls a hardy band of pigs turned over the topsoil. Remembering the story of his discovery as a baby he tied his horse and sat upon the wall and watched as they foraged among the roots of the almond trees.

While he watched the pigs at their work a small group of three mustachio'd bandits were watching him. When Mandorlinfiore noticed something silver glisten in the mud the bandits watched as he jumped down from his vantage point to retrieve whatever it may be.

'We'll have his horse while he's grubbing for truffles with the pigs,' the leader of the bandits declared, and at once they rode out of their hiding place, caught up his horse and were away before they could see what Mandorlinfiore had found. Indeed, in amongst the squabbling and squealing of the pigs Mandorlinfiore failed to hear the racket made by the horse-thieving bandits.

Mandorlinfiore had spent a good deal of time stock-checking and assessing and counting coin so he knew a fine piece of silver when he found one. What the pigs had uncovered was worth several horses and possibly even a payment on a new trading ship. Between the roots of the almond tree lay a hunting horn. He cleaned it with some rough grass and marvelled as the intricate patterns emerged. He imagined it had been lost by some eastern trader as it was so covered with curls and diamond shapes and what looked like words from some exotic language.

Imagine that you had found such a thing as this. Something that you knew had to make a noise if it was cleaned out and you put your lips to it. What would you do? I guess, correctly too I think, that you would attempt to make a noise. You would want to know what it sounded like wouldn't you? Well, that is exactly what Mandorlinfiore did, and do you know, the horn made such a horrible rasping noise that it silenced the pigs and the wind stood still.

At one end of the almond grove there was a little stream, and so Mandorlinfiore made for it to wash the traces of mud from the horn. As he dipped the instrument into the water dozens of tiny fish danced about his hands. The tinkling of the stream grew louder, and the tiny fish were gradually replaced with their slightly larger cousins.

When the horn was truly clean he shook the water out of it and lifted it to his lips. The sound that it made now would have brought an angel down to earth to reclaim it as his own.


## 9. A Bandit's Life is a Hard Life


You might think that a bandit's life is a hard life and you would be right. No one wants to give a bandit a job, no one wants a bandit to marry their daughter and no one wants a bandit for a neighbour. And so the bandits in this territory roamed from forest to mountain to swamp and hill looking for the end of their lives, for as everybody knows, there is no such thing as an old brigand. One or two might escape the life of a bandit and become an ordinary burglar, or a tax collector, or maybe go into the priesthood, but in the main, the ordinary bandit was a bandit because he could not abide a normal life.

The leader of the three mustachio'd bandits was considering retiring in a year or so, once he had enough loot to set up a small tax collecting office in Ajaccio. He was pleased with the new horse. He would trade it, he thought, it was not a mountain horse so would be no good in the terrain where he currently did most of his business. The other two bandits were younger and still full of fire, keen to fill their secret hideouts with booty. They were pleased with the fine saddle and other items strapped to the horse and were busy working out what prices they could get and how that would divide up, and how much more they would get once they had killed their leader and taken his share.

The leader knew what they were thinking because they were bandits and he had been as young as them once and had done the same thing many times, but he had a plan, and he would be ready.

They were not ready when Mandorlinfiore blew on his horn. The horses threw the three mustachio'd bandits onto the ground and turned about and galloped back up the mountain as fast as they could go. The three bandits fell and rolled down the steep mountainside until they came hard up against a huge boulder and all the wind was knocked out of them.

They struggled and fought to their feet and looked all around for their mounts, but they were not to be seen anywhere. It took them some time to regain the road and when they did it was apparent that their horses had ventured higher into the mountains.

'We must follow them and get them back,' said the leader, 'and kill the horse thief that took 'em!'

'Aye!' cheered his compatriots, and together they set off on foot, swords drawn.

*Bandits mean business.*

## 10. The Pig's Treasure

Well, there was our Mandorlinfiore, for the moment without a horse, but instead with a beautiful musical instrument. He went back to the spot where it had been found and inspected the place between the tree roots, drawing back the earth with a stick. It was then that he found a small chest, bound in iron with a lock in the shape of a heart. It was firmly stuck and he struggled to budge it. Just then, the friendly and curious mountain pigs came up to see what he was doing and, as they were experts at digging, they set to. Before long, Mandorlinfiore was able to prise the box free. When it was clear of the hole the pigs kept on with their digging, and began to bring up a hoard of gold coins.

After about five minutes it was clear that this was no small fortune and would easily pay for a fleet of merchant ships and the improvements to the harbour that would be required at Bonifacio. As he stood and marvelled at the industry of the pigs, he wondered how he would transport all of the gold.

A moment later his horse returned to him and his question was answered by the appearance of three more horses complete with saddlebags. He caught them all and led them to the stream where they drank their fill and settled on the grass in the afternoon sun. The pigs had completed their excavation of the hoard and had left a sizeable cave beneath the tree and a pyramid of gold in front of it. Mandorlinfiore began filling the saddlebags with the coins unaware that he was again being watched by the three mustachio'd bandits.

'See how he does our work for us,' said one.

'It will be fine houses and slaves for us with that gold,' said another.

'Wine and feasting will be the order of our days,' said the third.

They waited until all of the gold had been packed up in bags and then charged upon Mandorlinfiore, lifted him up and tied him to a tree. One went down and found the horses. He brought back wine from their saddles. Another gathered sticks and made a cooking fire while the third bandit caught and killed a pig.

They were all three very pleased with the way the day had turned out and were looking forward to a feast, and maybe some sport with the poor fellow they had trussed and tied when the leader of the bandits said, 'What sir, is in this chest? It must be precious indeed for it to be bound in iron so.'

'It is your heart's desire,' said Mandorlinfiore.

## 11. What is it that you seek?

Now then, a heart's desire could be many things. Whatever it is that your heart desires is bound to be different from that of your sister, or your neighbour, or even your husband or wife. Bandits on the other hand generally desire the same thing, that of mastery over others.

It could be argued that this is why they chose to tie Mandorlinfiore rather than just put him to the sword straightaway. It is also true to say that bandits also desire mastery over other bandits more than anything else.

The leader of our trio understood this and enjoyed ruling over his two compatriots. He was also wise enough to know that one day he would be too old to hold them back. He jabbed at the treasure chest with his sword, 'Where is the key to open it?' he said.

'On a chain about my horse's neck,' said Mandorlinfiore.

The bandit went to the horses to collect the key and after a futile search returned.

'It is not there,' he said to Mandorlinfiore, 'you lie.'

'No sir, I do not. The key must have fallen from my horse's neck when you took him down the mountain.'

The leader called his two compatriots to him and they discussed the situation. At first they tried to pick the lock, but it refused to budge. They tried putting the chest in the fire, but it was so bound in iron that it would not burn. At length it was decided that the two younger bandits would retrace their steps and seek out the key and chain while the leader stewed the pig.

Once the leader was alone with Mandorlinfiore he asked him what he was doing travelling these dangerous roads all alone.

'I am looking for something,' he said.

'I think you found it,' said the bandit, 'but it is a shame for you that I will have to put your neck to my sword later.'

'What will you do with all the gold?' asked Mandorlinfiore.

'I will buy a big house in Ajaccio and be a great man for the end of my days.' he said.

'And your compatriots? What will they do with their share?'

'They will surely gamble it all away in the end, or at the very beginning, try to kill me and take it all for themselves. I would have done the same once.'

Mandorlinfiore looked the old bandit square in the eye and said, 'I am the son of a merchant and well trained in the accounting of gold. If you spare my life I shall make sure you are not cheated out of your fortune.'

'Why would you do that?' said the bandit.

'In exchange for my life, sir. A fair trade I find.'

'And the gold?'

'I have no use for gold, sir. It is not gold that I seek.'

## 12. A Plot is Afoot

While Mandorlinfiore bargained with the devil for his own life, the two younger bandits were plotting their own wicked crime.

'You saw all that gold,' said one.

'Don't know what an old man would want with all that treasure,' said the other.

'He's so sure of himself,' said one.

'So high and mighty,' said the other.

And so, it went on all the way down the mountainside as they cast about for an invisible key on a not-there chain. At last they reached the place where they had been thrown from their horses and realised it had been getting dark.

'We'll never find the key in this light,' said one.

'Let's go back,' said the other, 'quick, too, before the old man gets the idea to go off and leave us here with no horses and no gold.'

'He wouldn't do that. We'd catch him and kill him.'

'Listen, with all that gold we could be fine men indeed.'

'We could?'

'We'd do proper things with the gold, like open the best betting house in Bonifacio!'

'With rooms upstairs?'

'And downstairs too.'

'The old man wouldn't like that. He'd want us to keep with him, keep all the gold in one place.'

'What about the rest of our loot?'

'I say we cut him down tonight.'

'Who?'

'The old man.'

And so it went on all the way back up the mountainside as they flashed their swords in the light of the rising moon.

## 13. The White Hart's Riddle

Now some people say that falling in love is an easy thing to do, while others maintain that love is something that must never be fallen into as it can hold a sting worse than nettles. Nonetheless, all around the world there are people falling in love every day, without a thought for where they might land.

The Princess Belfioré had always been of a mind to look before she leapt, indeed, one had to be especially careful in the precipitous terrain of Zonza. The morning of the day that she fell in love Belfioré had not the slightest inkling that she would.

When she looked out of her window there were no signs in the sky that would indicate today would be more propitious than most. There were no hints in the bubbles on her porridge and her old maid, who had been with her since birth, declared no strange sensations in either bones or water.

'What is your will today Milady?' said the old maid.

'I shall ride out into the forest. They say the White Hart has returned to the cliffs of the southern gorge,' said Belfioré.

'What will you do if you see him my dear?'

'I think I have an answer to his riddle,' said Belfioré.

'What's that?'

> *'I have two hands and five heads,*
> *Ten eyes and eighteen legs,*
> *Six chests and four tails,*
> *A hundred teeth and twenty nails.'*

'Sounds horrible,' the old maid shuddered, 'I shouldn't want to meet that in the forests of Zonza!'

Belfioré laughed, 'If the White Hart agrees that my answer is right, then I shall be able to tell you what it is.'

'Why can't you tell me now?'

'Because I am sworn to secrecy! I must not break the spell,' said Belfioré.

Well you might think that the existence of a riddle setting deer might be thought a little strange and, in most parts of the world, you would be right to think so, but this was the Kingdom of Zonza and there were still plenty of places left for such creatures to live. Nowadays, what with all the new towns and roads being built everywhere it is much harder to find a deer who can set a decent riddle.

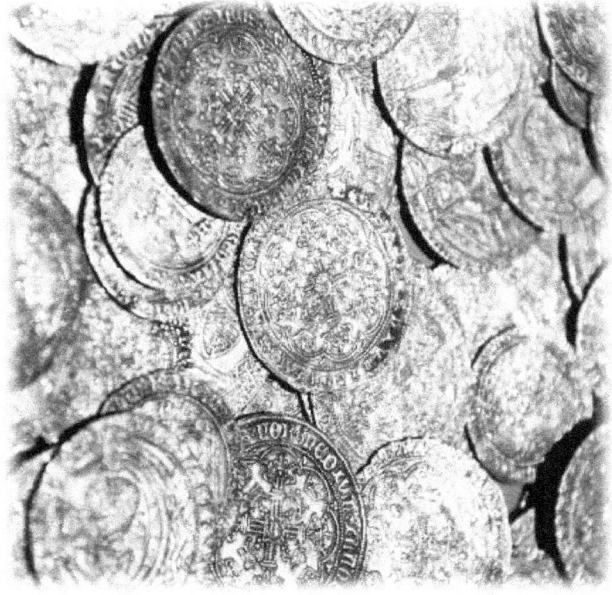

*Treasure trove.*

## 14. The Nature of Magic and Murder

A very long time ago a story started that is much older than our own, a story that not many of us ever get to hear as so many of us have forgotten what it was all about. The people who have not forgotten are the Mazerre who live deep in the Corsican Mountains. If you were to get on a bus to Zonza today, chances are you might get a seat next to a Mazerre. How would you know? It's easy. They smell of magic.

'Humbug!' I hear you say, 'Magic doesn't have a smell.'

Oh, but it does, and once you have caught its scent the memory of it will never leave you. But make no mistake for there are many tricksters out there eager to take your money, your heart, your time. The Mazerre do not smell of patchouli oil or rose water, or fish and chips. The smell of magic is far more subtle than that.

There was an odd scent blowing through the almond grove that night. The pig stew was nearly done, and the younger mustachio'd bandits were steeling their resolve as they crept closer under cover of darkness.

Then all at once they charged the old man and took off his head with both their swords at once. It rolled away and into the cave beneath the tree. They took the rest of his body and threw it after his head.

Then they turned to Mandorlinfiore who said, 'Thank goodness for that, the old man was plotting to kill us all while we slept!'

The two remaining mustachio'd bandits looked at each other and burst out laughing, 'Listen to him,' said one, 'he thinks now he is saved from the old man that he is safe with us!'

'I'm hungry,' said the other, 'let's eat this stew and then put him with the old man.'

And so, they took the stew and sat and ate like they had not had a meal for days, which, truth be told, they had not. While they gorged Mandorlinfiore quietly pulled at the ropes which held him to the tree.

When the bandits had had their fill, they leaned back by the cooking fire and held on to their bellies.

'I am so full I can hardly move,' said one.

'That must be because we had the old man's portion too,' said the other.

After a few minutes of happy grunting and belching, and other impolite goings on, a look of worry settled on both their faces.

'My hands have lost all feeling,' said one.

'I can't move my legs,' said the other.

After which they never said another word.


## 15. Set Free


If you have ever had to spend a night tied to a tree listening to the ghosts of three recently deceased mustachio'd bandits bicker about who murdered whom and why then you might have a good understanding of just how tired Mandorlinfiore was when the sun rose. As everybody knows ghosts vanish in sunlight but pigs awaken, run about, and size up whatever had been going on the night before.

Two pigs set about chewing on the ropes that held the captive close to the tree while the rest pushed the bodies of the two younger bandits into the cave beneath the tree before filling it in with dirt.

Mandorlinfiore went down to the stream, pulled out a fish for his breakfast and cooked it on a stick over the fire.

When he had finished eating he kicked over the cooking fire and pretty soon there was little left to tell of the events of last night.

As he was very grateful to be set free, he tickled the pigs until they squealed with delight. Then he rounded up the four horses and tied them together before loading them up with the bags of gold. He wanted to get away from the grove, and the bickering ghosts, as fast as he could.

He put the mysterious treasure chest in a saddle bag on his own horse, called his thanks to the mountain swine, and set off at a slow walk along the rutted road.

## 16. The Nature Of Time

You will forgive me because this is not a linear narrative, which means that time does not always go in straight lines while I am telling this story. The secret thing about time is that it is not as regular as your modern clocks would have you believe.

In this story time works as you would expect it to in real life, like a concertina. Sometimes everything will seem to happen all at once, while at other places in the story a week might go by for one character, while another simply has a very busy day.

This is all very well when we are dealing in small amounts of time, but we must still be careful and keep an eye on things. And remember, there are only a few of us who can go back, most, including you, may only go forwards through time.

For most of us I imagine time is like treacle and runs fast through the hot summer, slows through autumn, then stands absolutely still in the midst of winter while we wait and wait and wait for the spring thaw.

## 17. Late For a Wedding

You might think that after such an eventful start to his journey that Mandorlinfiore would by now be craving the comforts of home. He did think of his adoptive parents and how much good they could do with all of the gold he had acquired, but his quest to avenge his abandonment as a baby drove him on.

By the middle of the day he had left behind the cover of the trees and was high above the foothills of Zonza. From here he could see the thin sparkling ribbon that was the distant sea. This did give him some cause to think about his quest and while he was taking in the view and marvelling at the distance he had already covered there came the sound of a cowbell behind him.

'Ho traveller,' said a tall Moor. He led a huge white ox on a silver chain. 'I believe you have something of mine?'

'Good day sir,' said Mandorlinfiore, 'If you can name it you are welcome to it.'

'It is the Horn of Justice, the same horn that you found, cleaned and blew upon yesterday,' the Moor smiled a broad, satisfied grin, 'For the recovery of the horn I trust you were well rewarded?'

'Indeed, I was,' said Mandorlinfiore, and he reached inside his coat and took out the horn. He weighed it in the palm of his hand, 'it is a fine piece sir.'

'Should you find yourself in need of justice in the future, just clap, like this,' and the Moor clapped his hands three times, 'and say these words, Salamanca Salamanca.'

The horn vanished in front of Mandorlinfiore's eyes.

'Thank you, young man,' the Moor held the horn between finger and thumb.

'I don't understand?' said Mandorlinfiore, 'Why didn't you just clap your hands before?'

'I was trapped by the Mazerre for a hundred years,' said the Moor, 'They wanted this horn amongst other things. When you blew on the horn, I was freed. You must beware the Mazerre on your journey.'

'I am grateful for your warning sir,' said Mandorlinfiore.

'Now I must go,' said the Moor, 'I am late for a wedding,' and off he went, down the mountain road. Mandorlinfiore watched the Moor and his giant ox amble away and then started back on his own trek into the interior of Zonza.

*The rocky peaks of Zonza.*

## 18. A Story of Pizza

At the top of the first mountain pass into the heartlands of Zonza is an inn. It is not an ordinary inn. You can be very well assured that there is nothing ordinary in Zonza. It has been said that an inn has been on this site for three-thousand years, and that Julius Caesar once watered his horse here, and that the current innkeeper has kept the inn since it was first built.

The last may well be true as the innkeeper is no ordinary host, but is in fact, the King of the Animals. And so all the horses that stay in the stables are very well looked after, although the stable boys are never seen, and the restaurant and rooms for human guests, though sumptuous, are attended by invisible chambermaids, chefs and waiters.

The pizza at this particular inn is so absolutely delicious that you will never forget it. Whenever you hear the word 'pizza', or if someone you love suggests this meal, for ever after the memory of this most perfect example will automatically return. You will be in a top restaurant in one of the world's most sophisticated cities eating a pizza that has cost your host more than one hundred American dollars, and you will say, 'great pizza, but I had one in Corsica once, in this little place...'

No one knows the recipe. No one can match the flavours of the rippled cheese, the scorched tomatoes or the bright black olives, not even the world-famous experts in the kitchens of Napoli or New York can come close to this pizza. There is a very beautiful and sad story of a chef turned mad trying, but there is no time to tell it now, for here comes Mandorlinfiore.

'Good day innkeeper,' he said, 'I need shelter for myself and my horses.'

'Of course, sir,' said the innkeeper, and took hold of Mandorlinfiore's lead rein, 'and you will have pizza.'

'Thank you.'

## 19. The Nature of Death

Now it has been said before that the life of a bandit is usually shorter than most, and we have learned that they are just as likely to end each other's lives. You might think that a bandit's troubles would be over once put to the sword, or indeed poisoned. But you would be mistaken, for as is commonly known, a soul dispatched in an untimely or violent manner always has unfinished business.

Our three mustachio'd bandits were dead, but they were not gone. Mandorlinfiore had their horses, saddles and other possessions, and they had not finished with them.

One thing that bandits feared most of all was that after their untimely death, their secret hoards of treasure might be raided by other, less worthy bandits. Many bandits had once had a family they would prefer received the benefit of their hard-thieving days too. Others might want to atone for their sins by helping a priest discover their gold. By the time the sun had set a second time, our bandits had found an accord and had set off to catch up with Mandorlinfiore.

It would be fair to say that when you are alive, ghosts and magical beings are very difficult to recognise as such as they are very good at camouflage or invisibility.

If, however, you have ever been dead, then you will know that, being dead, everything, and everyone, is far more visible. You can see the tree spirits, the water sprites and the old Roman ghosts sitting on a bend in the road.

When the three mustachio'd bandits made it to the inn, they could see from the doorway that it was crammed full of people. There was a waiter at every table, whether there was a party at the table or not, and there were sweepers picking up dust, and barmen polishing glasses.

At one end of the bar they could see a small stage, upon which sat five rather familiar mustachio'd bandits with guitars.

'This is the inn of the dead?' said one mustachio'd bandit.

'The inn of ghosts? I never heard of such a place,' said another.

Then the leader of the three mustachio'd bandits said, 'Do you not recognise this place? We rode past here just two days ago and it was empty.'

'There was no-one to rob,' said the first mustachio'd bandit.

'That's right,' said the other.

'And one of you youngsters had a dream that if we were to come here we would be lost,' said the leader, 'and you know, there is a legend that this innkeeper is King of the Animals and will cheat you out of your life.'

'Look there,' said one, 'it's our horse thief.'

'He looks very happy,' said the other.

'That's because he's spending all our gold.' said one, 'Let's get him!'

And so, the two younger mustachio'd bandits charged into the bar with their swords drawn.

20. A Dangerous Enchantment

Mandorlinfiore had set himself in a wicker chair in the shade with a view down the pass and across the interior of Zonza. The next valley was thickly forested and surrounded by high, steep granite mountains.

There was the tinkling of glasses on the table next to him. A beautiful jug brimming with cold water appeared with a small cup. Mandorlinfiore poured some water and drank it quickly.

As he was finishing his third glass of water his pizza arrived. He ate it slowly, marvelling at every bite. While he ate, he listened to a mariachi band that, he assumed, must have been playing in the next room. The mariachis played songs of melancholic love that were not at all unpleasant. Afterwards, the innkeeper showed him to his room.

'Your ghosts have met some old friends,' said the innkeeper, 'and have promised to leave you alone tonight.'

'My what?' said Mandorlinfiore, 'I have no ghosts.'

The innkeeper said nothing. Mandorlinfiore, too tired to question any further, had a wash and then fell into bed to have a long and deep and dreamless sleep.

Meanwhile, our three mustachio'd bandits had discovered murder and mayhem amongst their former gang members.

'You killed him because he killed Pedro so then you were killed by Juan?' said one of our three mustachio'd bandits.

'That's right,' said one of the five mustachio'd bandits as he strummed his guitar, 'and then we all ended up here. We didn't mean to, and I guess it's not so bad, but I think we might get a bit bored after a while.'

'Why don't you just get up and leave?' asked the other mustachio'd bandit.

'Oh well,' said another of the guitar playing mustachio'd bandits, 'we tried that, but this place is cursed.'

'What do you mean?' said the leader of the three mustachio'd bandits.

'It's like this,' said another mustachio'd bandit, who had been playing a trumpet up until a moment ago, 'you get here, dead or alive, and accept some kind act of hospitality from the esteemed inn-keeper, and before you know it, here you are.'

'I don't understand,' said all three mustachio'd bandits.

'If you are alive, and spend three nights here, then you will remain forever and invisible to any human eye,' said the trumpet playing bandit, 'if you are already dead do not expect to be able to leave after second sun-up.'

'Then we must leave now,' said the leader of the three mustachio'd bandits.

'No. You must wait until the hour before first light, for that is the hour that the King of the Animals' servants' sleep. Rouse your horses and your master then.'


## 21. Escape Thwarted


And so, the three mustachio'd bandits sat and waited for the servants of the King of the Animals to fall asleep. While they waited, they caught up with news from the other bandits and played cards, each trying to out-cheat the other.

When the five mustachio'd mariachi bandits suddenly fell to sleep the other three jumped up, rifled their pockets and then dashed out to the stables. The two younger bandits woke the horses while the older bandit went for Mandorlinfiore.

Now it has not been said before in this tale so I suppose that I must confirm your suspicions; that a ghostly bandit who had lost his life when he had lost his head now has the inconvenience of having to carry his head under his arm.

In the bedroom of Mandorlinfiore he stood and held his head close to that of our hero.

'Awake, awake! We must escape!' said the mustachio'd bandit.

'What? Is there a fire?' mumbled Mandorlinfiore.

'Worse than that,' cried the mustachio'd bandit, 'there is enchantment that will make you a slave!'

'Ha! You will have to do better than that bandit!' said Mandorlinfiore, 'I will leave when I am ready to leave and not a moment before!'

'If you stay one more night then you will not be able to leave. The inn-keeper is the King of the Animals and he will have you under his spell!' The mustachio'd bandit was waving his head around in a very distracted manner.

'Keep still,' said Mandorlinfiore, 'you are making me dizzy.'

'Sorry,' mumbled the mustachio'd bandit, 'I just do not want to remain here forever watching you wait at table in silence and invisible.'

'I am still not convinced that you mean well bandit,' said Mandorlinfiore.

'Please sir, call me Escobar,' said the mustachio'd bandit.

'Very well Escobar,' said Mandorlinfiore, 'and your robber brothers?'

'They are Fabio and Sandrino,' said Escobar.

'And where are they?'

'We are here sir,' said Fabio.

'We could not wake the horses,' said Sandrino.

'It is first light already,' said Escobar, 'tonight you must not sleep if you want to escape.'

'I will leave after breakfast this very morning,' said Mandorlinfiore, 'one night in a soft bed is enough for any man on a quest.'

*Mustachio'd Bandit.*

## 22. The White Hart

Belfioré knew the winding paths to the Southern Gorges better than any of the King's men. Even though the King regularly dispatched his knights to follow his beloved daughter into the wild places of Zonza, they could seldom keep up.

Many times, they would simply wait to see her return safely at some good vantage point rather than become lost. This was not to say that the King's men were not loyal and brave knights rather that they were used to the curious ways of the Princess.

Had they been able to match her prowess in the saddle as she galloped along ledges hand-span wide and leaped gorges deeper than forever, then they too would have been heroes of legend.

But this is not their story.

And the White Hart was not a creature that suffered the trials of men. He stood alone on a high rock outcrop. From here he could see the clouds forming and watch the snow crystals come together in the air.

He snorted and blew steam out of his nose, stamped a front hoof and shook his head.

There was a chance that the Princess might have the answer to his riddle. He was confident that it was a very difficult riddle. He would be very surprised if she had worked it out but pleased all the same.

The riddle had come to him when he was sleeping and dreaming of the future. This riddle meant something. It was a window into the Princess's fate. If she had solved it then it would tell her something very important.

He snorted and stamped again. It felt as though she was late, but he had not set a time; perhaps it was simply his own impatience.

Then suddenly, there came the unmistakeable sound of iron on stone. Belfioré had entered the gorge.

## 23. Pancakes

As soon as he had dressed for the day and entered the restaurant breakfast was laid out ready for Mandorlinfiore. There were pancakes and strawberries, lemon juice, honey and a jug of orange juice.

Mandorlinfiore sat down and began to eat. He chopped the strawberries and poured honey and lemon over them, then rolled up the pancake to make a delicate parcel of the whole thing.

Escobar, Fabio and Sandrino watched from the door. They might now be invisible to you and I in the light of day, but the innkeeper, as has been told before, was not like you and I.

'Bandits!' he snapped, 'I have work for you.'

'But we are dead,' said Escobar, 'how can we work?'

'I am the King of the Animals and can do many things. You will sort my grains of rice for me.'

'I have heard of this,' whispered Sandrino, 'we will be sorting rice grains for all eternity.'

'We must refuse,' said Escobar, 'for we have unfinished business and must be on our way.'

'I see,' said the innkeeper, 'but I understand that your unfinished business is eating pancakes at my table.'

'He is a small part of it your Highness,' said Fabio, 'we have done banditry right across the island of Corsica and must see to all sorts of business.'

'But see how your man devours the pancakes?'

'We do,' said Escobar, 'they look like good pancakes.'

'Oh, they are,' said the innkeeper, 'magical pancakes.'

'What do you mean?' said Escobar,

'You might as well leave now,' said the innkeeper, 'with food this good your man will want to stay here forever.'

'That cannot be!' said Sandrino.

'No! Mandorlinfiore is on a quest!' said Fabio.

'We'll see,' said the innkeeper, 'there were many souls that were 'on a quest' when they stopped in here for pizza or pancakes. Now they realise that a pancake or a pizza is all you need.'

'Then we must go,' said Escobar, and dragged his protesting compatriots out into the road.

## 24. What Are You Afraid Of?

It is said by some who think they know that the Mazerre of Corsica is a tribe which is older than mankind.

It is also said by others that the Mazerre fell out of heaven when God and Lucifer, the Devil to you and me, had their big argument. They hid in the mountains of Corsica and waited for it all to die down. Of course, it never has.

Wherever the Mazerre are from, their shadows remain on the island to this day, walking through city streets or wandering high mountain passes. In the days when our story is set, they would commonly be seen about and not be concerned about us seeing their true nature. Today things are far more complicated.

The three mustachio'd bandits continued to bicker by the side of the road. Mandorlinfiore was most of their unfinished business and as such could not be abandoned to the King of the Animals.

A plan would have to be set, but what that plan could possibly be none could agree upon.

'We need help,' said Escobar.

'What sort of help?' said Fabio.

'We need a Mazerre,' said Escobar.

'No way,' cried Fabio, 'that would be like setting a crocodile to catch a crocodile.'

'The Mazerre would take Mandorlinfiore for himself,' said Sandrino.

'Oh no,' said Escobar, 'not when we have something interesting to trade.'

'I don't care what you have to trade,' said Fabio, 'we cannot get mixed up with the Mazerre, things are bad enough already.'

'Fabio is right,' said Sandrino, 'you will burn down the house to save the chicken shed.'

'What are you afraid of?' said Escobar.

'Why are you not afraid?' said Sandrino, 'Just because you are dead does not mean you are safe from the magic that is in the world.'

'You are right,' said Escobar, 'we must find some other way.'


## 25. A Riddle Solved

*'I have two hands and five heads,*
*Ten eyes and eighteen legs,*
*Six chests and four tails,*
*A hundred teeth and twenty nails,'*

'I thought it was perhaps a woman riding a horse and leading three others but,' Belfioré hesitated, 'I could not work out what the sixth chest could be unless it was a treasure chest?'

'You are almost right Princess,' said the White Hart, 'but my answer is not a woman.'

'A man? A Prince, a Lord or a Knight with a treasure chest?' said Belfioré, 'Not another one.'

'No Princess,' said the White Hart, 'not another one. Simply a man. But he carries with him something very special, he has no idea that he carries it with him, but if he is found out he will be in mortal danger.'

'And what has this to do with me?' asked Belfioré.

'He needs your help,' said the White Hart, 'he is at the inn of the King of the Animals.'

'Is this another riddle?' said Belfioré.

'Oh no,' said the White Hart, 'I am being very serious. You must ride there now with your King's Men and free him from the enchantment of the King of the Animals.'

'But how can I do that?' asked Belfioré.

'Go to the place, the inn, and call the King of the Animals and set him this riddle;

*I am older than the wind,*
*I was here before the sun,*
*Sooner than the river run,*
*before time was begun,*
*What am I?*

'But what does it mean?' said Belfioré.

'Don't worry,' said the White Hart, 'the King of the Animals will take until dawn to work it out, by which time you will be gone.'

'Thank you, White Hart,' and so Belfioré turned her horse and set off back up the gorge at a gallop, happy to have worked out one riddle, and pleased to be set an adventure.

## 26. Water and Wood

Now as it has been discussed before, when a person becomes dead then particular things become revealed to them, such as the futility of some mortal pre-occupations, and the extraordinary prevalence of nature spirits.

Every tree has a Dryad, or tree spirit, which is why some folk like to hug trees from time to time, and all streams and rivers teem with water nymphs. A woodland walk could become a very sociable event for a ghost.

Close by the inn run by the King of the Animals was a dense stretch of forest. Escobar led the way and was soon in conversation with a Dryad. Well, when I say conversation, what I mean is that talking to the trees is very different from talking to people.

'That King of the Animals eh?' said Escobar, 'Thinks he's so great.'

'Chopping us up for winter he does,' said the Dryad, 'charcoaling for ovens, not old, not fallen, but all.'

'He's a bad'un for sure,' said Escobar, 'and needs a lesson.'

'Lesson yes, lesson,' said the Dryad, 'lesson less trees left with charcoaling and chopping, lesson him yes.'

'But you have magic, don't you?' said Escobar.

'Old magic, magic as old as the old ones,' said the Dryad, 'old and slow. Slower than the axe, slower than fire.'

'But strong,' said Escobar, 'your magic is very strong.'

'Slower than time,' said the Dryad, 'but does not need time.'

Escobar's mustachio twitched. He had an idea.

'Listen to me Dryad,' he said, 'this is what we will do, and lesson we will teach to the King of the Animals.'

'Good,' said the Dryad, and his tree shivered.

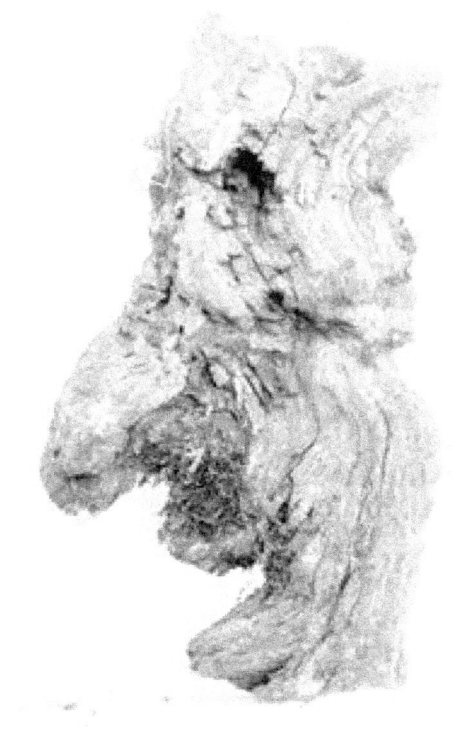

*Old Oaken-face.*

## 27. More Pancakes

Mandorlinfiore had forgotten about the three mustachio'd bandits. He had forgotten about all the gold he had in his saddlebags. He had forgotten about the quest to find his true parents.

All he could think about was pancakes. He had pancakes with lemon juice, he had pancakes with lime juice, and he poured honey over pancakes and sprinkled chopped strawberries on top.

When his plate was empty an invisible waiter was ready with another pancake. He spread cream and jam and grated apple and finely ground salt over his pancakes and once he was served a pancake with bacon and a fried egg. To go with his breakfast feast he had orange juice with ice topped with slices of lemon and lime. All the while another invisible attendant dabbed the mess away from his cheeks. You might think that gorging on pancakes at breakfast time is a fantastic idea, and indeed there can be no finer way to set yourself up for the day. I may recommend one or two pancakes but Mandorlinfiore had just finished his thirty-sixth when his belt began to feel a little tight.

But that did not stop him taking a thirty-seventh pancake when it was offered. He made a satisfied kind of grunt when he forked the first mouthful, and then stopped.

An image of a mountain pig came into his mind and a tear ran down his cheek. He put down his knife and fork and looked about the restaurant.

The sun was low in the sky. He had been eating breakfast all day long. The innkeeper was watching him with a satisfied smile on his face.

Mandorlinfiore frowned and tried to hold on to the image of the mountain pig and work out what it meant. He loosened his belt and rested his elbows on the table. The pancake on his plate looked and smelled wonderful. He wanted to eat it.

So he did.

## 28. A Forest on the March

As night began to fall on the mountains of Zonza, and the mariachi band of mustachio'd bandits struck up their mournful tunes, while Mandorlinfiore started on his forty-fourth pancake and a Princess and her guards galloped along the road, an old magic was working once again.

Earth and stones crumbled as roots loosened and the trees rose up from the forest floor. Rocks were scattered down the mountainside to block brooks and streams, to alter their course and make new ponds and pools.

It is said that a particular waterfall, beloved by poets and lovers alike, was formed the night the Dryads took on the King of the Animals.

When trees sway in a strong breeze a forest can look like it is on the move, but it is nothing like the sight of trees walking across the earth.

These fir trees were not like your little Christmas trees that fit snugly in your house at Christmas. They were not even like the Christmas trees you might see in the town square. No, these trees were taller than the town hall.

Oak trees and chestnut trees joined the firs as they marched upon the inn. At the head of the forest army were our three mustachio'd bandits. They ran in to free Mandorlinfiore's horses with young Dryad saplings who were keen to make a proper adventure of it.

They whipped the horses out of their oat fuelled stupor and they were soon on their feet and ready to go. Their whinnies were answered by the calls of other horses by the road at the front of the inn.

The Princess had arrived with the King's men to rescue Mandorlinfiore. They clattered up to the front terrace where their horses snorted and blew steam.

'What is the meaning of this?' cried the innkeeper, 'This is an esteemed establishment we have here.'

Then he saw the Princess Belfioré. He recognised her immediately, 'Your Highness,' he bowed low, 'you look famished.'

## 29. A Battle Begins

Trees do not march swiftly, but they march with irresistible purpose, which means that nothing can get in their way. They tore down the wall of the innkeeper's compound; they crushed the stone outbuildings and returned the terraced gardens to their natural slope.

When they reached the inn the trees encircled it like an oak stockade. The ghosts and enchanted persons in thrall to the King of the Animals had been herded into a tight ring around the inn.

In the restaurant the King of the Animals had no idea what was going on outside. He was himself enchanted by the beauty of Belfioré and he bowed and scraped and begged for her to be served by him at his very best table.

Belfioré was hungry it was true, but when she saw Mandorlinfiore snoring into his plate, she realised that this was the man that the White Hart had sent her to save.

'Innkeeper,' she said, 'I understand that you are his Highness the King of the Animals.'

'Ah Princess,' he said, 'I have been compared to that scoundrel from time to time, but I am only a simple innkeeper.'

'I am sure...' started Belfioré, when there was a deafening crash from one end of the restaurant as the ceiling fell in.

'What is this?' roared the innkeeper, and he began to transform before Belfioré's eyes. His legs grew longer, his breeches ripped apart to reveal dark fur covering his knees. Horns sprouted from his head.

A great tree trunk crashed through the wall and the roof above began to sag heavily.

'I will not have it!' snorted the innkeeper, who was now revealed as the King of the Animals, and was at least as tall as the inn, and getting taller.

'We must leave,' said Belfioré to the King's men, 'take this man and put him on my horse.'

Just then Escobar, Fabio and Sandrino charged into the restaurant with Mandorlinfiore's four horses. Escobar held his head high, 'Leave him to us Majesty.'

'These are his horses,' said Belfioré, 'how they come to us on their own is unknown, but fortunate. Load him onto his horse.'

'We are his ghosts,' said Escobar, 'we must do it.'

'Escobar,' said Sandrino, 'the Princess cannot hear you. We are not her ghosts.'

Above them the roof of the building was being torn apart. The King of the Animals had grown to the size of the largest pine tree.

'We have to go now,' said Belfioré.

## 30. Magic Un-Made

The King's Men piled Mandorlinfiore onto his own horse and the party fled the restaurant. The stockade of trees parted, and they galloped in the direction of the City of Zonza.

They were followed out by a stream of ghosts and once enchanted people, who were regaining their former solidity and sense.

Above them the King of the Animals roared and cursed, stamped and snorted. He caught up some of the smaller trees and sent them spinning over the top of the rampaging forest.

The trees fought back, closing the circle and turning the inn to dust beneath their roots. They sought to crush the King of the Animals too and return him to the earth he came from.

For every tree the King of the Animals hurled to the back of the massed timber ranks he lost another square of ground. He raised himself up to twice the height of the tallest fir, but still they closed around him.

It is said that there is nothing more dangerous than a cornered animal, and the King of the Animals possessed all of the wiles and cunning, venom and snarl of the most fearsome creatures that roamed the earth.

With one leap he cleared the crush of trees and landed square in the road ahead of Belfioré and the column of refugees.

'Aha!' he bellowed, 'So you want to take on the most powerful of the ancient Kings?'

The company's horses stood absolutely still as if frozen to the spot, which they were.

'Once the old trees have had their fun and gone back to sleep I will clap my hands and you will all return to your places in my re-made inn!' roared the King of the Animals, 'But first I think I must make the Princess pay!'

Belfioré dismounted and stepped forward. The King's men protested but she signalled for them to be silent. Mandorlinfiore continued to snore.

'Your Highness,' she said, 'may I speak with you?'

The King of the Animals clapped his hands once and returned to human size. 'What is it Princess?' he said.

*'I am older than the wind,*
*I was here before the sun,*
*Sooner than the river run,*
*Before time was begun,*
*What am I?'*

## 31. Saved

The King of the Animals at once sat down on a rock beside the road and began scratching his beard. 'I know it, I know it, I know it,' he muttered, 'I know it, I know it, I know it.'

'If you cannot think of the answer now then I must leave you to work it out,' said Belfioré, 'My soldiers are tired and need to rest after a long day and it is still a few hours in the saddle before we reach the next inn.'

'Give me a clue Princess,' said the King of the Animals, 'If you leave now all of my work at the inn will be undone. I will have to start again.'

'You will never be in business in Zonza again,' said the Princess.

'Your riddle has made me a prisoner, but I will solve it Princess, and I will have my revenge,' grumbled the King of the Animals.

'I'll be ready,' Belfioré narrowed her eyes, 'anytime you want to try.'

She turned about and climbed back on her horse. The company of King's Men, ghosts and other folk cheered and followed Belfioré deeper into the royal forests of Zonza.

It is said that the King of the Animals went back into the inn business and that he continues to provide perfect pizzas and impossible pancakes to all who come through his door. It is also said that it is quite safe to eat at his restaurant as long as you can resist the "All You Can Eat" offer.

Thanks to the actions of Belfioré and the ghost of the bandit Escobar there were many happy reunions for people presumed missing or dead, although some had, by means of the enchantment, out-lived their friends by many hundreds of years, which is another story altogether.

Belfioré raced home and was able to get to the Castle of Zonza in time for porridge and her usual chat with the King. She knew her Father would have been furious had he heard of her exploits the day before, and that she had been out all night.

The King's Men reported to the Sergeant at Arms and delivered Mandorlinfiore, his horses and his ghosts to the stables just inside the castle walls.

## 32. The Castle Of Zonza

What is a castle? Some say it is a strong room for all of the treasure of a Kingdom. Others say it is a barracks for all of the soldiers in a Kingdom. Some see a castle as a place to go to buy and sell goods.

Few see a castle as a family home, and the Castle of Zonza certainly worked hard not to give that impression. Its walls were made of hard black granite, forged in prehistoric volcanoes and impossible to breach with a cannonball.

There was a tall tower at the centre of the castle from which, it was said, all of the lands belonging to the Kingdom of Zonza, could be seen. As the castle was built on a high peak in the middle of the Valley of Zonza, this might well have been true.

These days no-one is quite sure of the exact location of the Castle of Zonza. It may have been here, it may have been there, but in the time in which our story is set there is no mistaking it.

Some castles, because of the landscape, require great earthworks or moats in order to make them secure. The Castle of Zonza managed with the dangerous rocky outcrops and sheer drops.

It might seem from what you are hearing that the Princesses' home was an unpleasant place to be; far from it. The tall windows let in the pure mountain light which lit up tapestries and painted banners on every wall.

The King of Zonza also had an enthusiasm for music from all quarters of the Kingdom and there were minstrels and mariachi strumming and tootling and chanting at all hours of the day.

The Queen of Zonza was less impressed, but then very little seemed to brighten her days other than the promise of a journey to the mainland.

The Princess of Zonza had known no other castle and presumed all to be alike, and so harboured no desire to travel hundreds of miles and cross dangerous seas to see them. Especially as she had met a good deal of the Princes and Lords and Knights that lived in them, and we already know what she thought of them.

The stables were well looked after by the head groom and smelled of fresh hay. This morning they also smelled of stale pancakes.

## 33. An Audience with the King

Mandorlinfiore awoke with a sore head. He had had a number of strange dreams since arriving at the inn and was glad to feel awake once more.

The smell of fresh hay was remarkably pleasant and revived him a little. He wiped the sleep from his eyes and looked about.

'What a peculiar thing it is to dream,' he said to himself, 'walking trees and cheeky ghosts, how ridiculous. I must have had too much cheese on my pizza. But I do not remember making my bed in the stable.'

He stood up and straight away saw his four horses comfortable in their stalls. The saddles and saddle bags were stacked in neat rows and the bridles and reins were hung and polished.

'Such good attention from my host,' remarked Mandorlinfiore, 'I must thank whoever has worked so hard.'

'Good morning sir,' said one of the King's Men, 'now I see that you are awake I have been asked to take you to the King.'

'The King is here at the inn?' said Mandorlinfiore.

'No sir, these are the Royal stables of the King of Zonza,' said the King's Man, 'now follow me.'

The King was waiting at the stable door upon a fine black stallion, 'My daughter tells me that you are here as the answer to some riddle or other,' said the King, 'what do you know of riddles?'

'Nothing sire,' said Mandorlinfiore, 'I am a merchant's adopted son and simply know the value of gold.'

'Indeed,' said the King, 'I hear you have a fine collection in your saddlebags. Did you steal it from me?'

'No sire, I came upon it fairly and I would return it to my parents when I discover who they are,' said Mandorlinfiore.

'Aha!' exclaimed the King, 'So you are a riddle after all. Go to my counting house and find out why my gold leaks out of it and you may keep your saddlebags for your parents. Refuse and I shall have your head and your gold.'

'Then I shall go at once to your counting house Sire,' said Mandorlinfiore, 'and I will find and stop the leak for you.'

'Good decision young man,' said the King, 'I'm certain that we will get along very well.'


## 34. The Counting House


Mandorlinfiore grumbled all the way to the counting house. He had no idea how he had managed to get into such a pickle, and less idea of how he might get out of it. At the door he met the King's Treasurer. He carried a very large set of keys. 'I am the King's Gaoler too,' he said by way of introduction, 'and I lock up any the King fancies is stealing from him.'

'After you lock them up,' asked Mandorlinfiore, 'does the gold stop going missing?'

'No.'

'I see, I am Mandorlinfiore and the King has asked me to help.'

'I know,' said the Treasurer, 'although I can't see what you can do for him. You can call me Treasurer for now, but I expect you'll be calling me Gaoler before too long.'

The counting house was built into the granite mountain with walls no cannonball could ever break down. Two guards stood outside the main door and two inside.

The Treasurer took Mandorlinfiore along a passage which had thick oak doors, bound in iron, set into the walls. At the end of the passage a guard kept watch on the huge strong room door.

On the door was a massive lock and the Treasurer had to use both hands to turn it. 'This is the gold room,' he said, 'you need not worry about what is behind the other doors, it is only the gold behind this door that goes missing.'

'But it looks to me that your dungeons could not be less well guarded,' said Mandorlinfiore.

'Indeed,' said the Treasurer.

Mandorlinfiore looked about the room. The walls, floor and ceiling were smooth polished granite. Upon the floor were stacked wooden chests in neat rows.

At the centre of the room was a desk lit by an oil lamp. Upon the desk there sat a heavily bound accounting book, and a cat.

'The task is beyond me,' said the Treasurer, 'I fear that you are the only thing standing between me and the gallows.'

'Fear not,' said Mandorlinfiore, 'for I know gold very well. Bring me a bed and three meals a day and I will soon have this accounting book fixed.'

## 35. To Work

As we have seen before in our story a ghost is not seen abroad in daylight very much, but in the dim light of the counting house strong room Escobar, Sandrino and Fabio were quite visible.

'I have never seen so many treasure chests,' said Escobar, 'there must be more gold here than in any other place in the world!'

'I am faint at the thought,' said Sandrino.

'Be quiet,' said Mandorlinfiore, but the Treasurer had left and there was no chance of the guard hearing their talk through the enormous door, 'we need to begin counting all of the gold in the chests.'

Mandorlinfiore first counted the treasure chests. There were fifty-two stacked all around the room. He chose one and pried open the lid.

It was empty.

He opened the next one and the next one and found that they were empty too. Once he had opened ten chests and found them all to be empty, he began to worry.

When twenty-two chests had been opened and proven to be empty, he began to fear for his life. Then the twenty-third chest proved to be full, as did all the rest.

Mandorlinfiore dragged all of the empty chests to one side and began counting the gold from one full chest into an empty one. That way he kept track of the gold so that he could not count any twice.

He marked the chests he had counted with a chalk cross and a number and then entered his sums in the ledger on the desk. All the while the ghosts chattered, drunk on the sight of so much gold.

The cat watched Mandorlinfiore inscribe the great book with his quill, 'Such neat handwriting,' said the cat, 'the King likes neat handwriting.'

'You talk?' said Mandorlinfiore.

The cat narrowed its eyes, 'You count,' it said, 'which I think is more surprising, especially for your kind.'

'My kind?' said Mandorlinfiore.

'Is he always this stupid?' the cat addressed the ghosts, and they nodded, 'Then the King will have his head too, just like the others.'

'No! No!' cried Escobar, 'He has unfinished business. He is a clever man but not used to the ways of the world. Can you help us?'

*Granite mountains as old as time.*

## 36. What a Cat Knows

The cat turned its back on Mandorlinfiore and the three mustachio'd bandits and began washing its paws. Mandorlinfiore reached out to stroke it but its tail was twitching so he thought better of it.

'Master Cat, sir,' started Mandorlinfiore, 'I did not mean to cause offence, but no cat I have ever met before has deemed me fit company to speak to.'

The cat stopped its washing, turned to Mandorlinfiore and said, 'I can well believe that.' Then stood and stretched and said, 'What in all of Zonza are you doing here?'

'I am here to account for the King's gold,' said Mandorlinfiore, 'he seems to think that this strong room leaks.'

'Then the King would be right. At midnight tonight you will see why, but how you can stop such a leak is beyond me,' said the cat, 'and I am a very intelligent cat indeed.'

'Master!' said Sandrino, 'Look here!'

Sandrino was on his knees in a corner of the room. He was pointing at a gold coin lodged in a crack in the stone wall.

'Escobar,' said Mandorlinfiore, 'tell me what is behind this wall.'

'How do I do that sir?' said Escobar.

'You are a ghost Escobar, surely a solid wall is no barrier to you now?' said Mandorlinfiore.

'I will go,' said Sandrino, 'I do not believe there can be a fate worse than death.'

'We must keep hold of you Sandrino,' said Fabio, 'I do not want to be left behind with these two.'

And so it was that Sandrino stepped into the wall while Fabio held onto his belt. Then Fabio too passed through the stone while Escobar held on. Soon only Escobar's head remained in the strong room, held aloft like a lantern.

'If your ghosts had an ounce of brain they would most likely be terribly dangerous,' purred the cat.

'What would you know of ghosts cat?' said Mandorlinfiore.

'Not Master Cat, sir, anymore?' said the cat, 'For shame. But then the manners of men will always fall short. When your idiot ghosts come out of the rock they will tell you it is solid because they have entered the wall several feet from the floor.'

'And your point, mister cat sir,' said Mandorlinfiore.

'My point is that what you are looking for is much closer to your feet than your head.'

At that moment Fabio and Sandrino returned shaking their heads.

'Solid rock?' said Mandorlinfiore.

'Solid rock,' said Sandrino.

'Escobar?' said Mandorlinfiore.

'Yes?' said Escobar.

'Put your head through the rock by the coin and tell me what you see,' said Mandorlinfiore.

Escobar did as he was told. He held his head in both hands and was in and out in moments.

'There is a passage, with steps leading down,' said Escobar.

'Can you see how the door opens?' said Mandorlinfiore.

'I must look again,' said Escobar, and his head disappeared into the wall once more.

A minute later he returned. 'There is a lever behind a panel just here,' said Escobar, 'if you push down gently the door will open.'

Mandorlinfiore did as he was shown, and a small door swung silently open. It was half the height of a man and narrow too.

## 37. A Secret Passage

Mandorlinfiore pushed a wooden chest into the opening to hold it open. It looked very dark inside the passage, so he took an oil lamp from the desk in order to see better.

'I'll go first,' said Escobar, which he did. Mandorlinfiore, bent double, followed. Fabio and Sandrino brought up the rear.

The light from the oil lamp shone through the ghost of the mustachio'd bandit. The walls were polished black granite, smooth to the touch.

The steps were steep and also worn so smooth that Mandorlinfiore had to concentrate hard so that he did not slip.

The deeper they went, the warmer it seemed to get, and as they descended the stairs a peculiar humming sound grew louder.

'Put out your light,' said Escobar.

Mandorlinfiore did as he was told. Instead of the pitch black he expected there was a rich golden glow rising up the stairs from an archway at the bottom.

'What can it be?' said Mandorlinfiore.

'I will go and take a look,' said Escobar, and so he crept down the last few steps until his feet were level with the top of the arch. Then he carefully lowered his head in his hands so he could peek below it.

## 38. Of Fire and Gold

It has been said by many great and learned scholars of these matters that wherever people get together in the world to share stories there will always be stories of magical winged fire-breathing creatures.

Our cousins in China have an entire year dedicated to the dragon. In Japan dragons also play an important part. The island nation of England has a story of a patron saint who rescues a Princess from such a creature.

The English share this story with the people of Greece who decorate the walls of their churches with the famous scene of Saint George's victory over the beast.

What the history books will not tell you about Saint George is that he did not indeed kill any dragon, but instead he made a bargain with it.

You see, dragons are the natural descendants of the dinosaurs. Had it not been for the catastrophe of the Bay of Mexico then dinosaurs would still be Masters of the Earth.

Instead, that is now our destiny, and we must take care of our responsibilities.

Dragons, as many people are aware, are fiercely intelligent creatures and, having survived for so many millennia, are determined not to be found out.

Unfortunately, they also have a weakness that has proved many a dragon's undoing. This weakness, as you probably know, is for gold.

Escobar also had a weakness for gold, and so, when he saw the great piles of coins shining in the light of a dragon's breath, he let out a little yelp, and dropped his head.

Instinctively Mandorlinfiore jumped down and ran to rescue Escobar's head as it tumbled away, but the bandit's bonce bounced down the steps and out into a great cavern.

It eventually came to rest next to the tip of a nasty looking claw.

Escobar's body, drawn by the supernatural ghostly elastic that connects dismembered parts in the next life, ran after his head and snatched it up.

The dragon opened a heavy-lidded eye and peered down at Mandorlinfiore.

'A visitor,' it said, 'how nice to have a visitor. Not related to that dreadful George I hope?'

## 39. What's In a Name?

'Good Day dragon,' said Mandorlinfiore, who had heard the story of Saint George, but never taken it seriously.

'And a good day to you too human,' returned the dragon, 'although I should not be upset by your not knowing my name.'

'I am Mandorlinfiore, at your service.'

'Mandorlinfiore,' repeated the dragon, 'how nice. Now I wonder if you can guess my name.'

'Guess?'

'Oh, please do. That would be lovely. I decided to call myself something new today, just for a change.'

It was quite clear to Mandorlinfiore that this particular dragon had probably not been out very much recently or had many people to talk to.

Escobar whispered in his ear.

'Goldentail?' said Mandorlinfiore.

'Nice, but no,' said the dragon, 'two more guesses then I'll have to eat you.'

'Two more guesses and then you'll eat me?' said Mandorlinfiore.

'That wasn't a very good guess,' said the dragon, 'I'll let that one go, but you really must think harder. We dragons are very particular about what we call ourselves.'

Mandorlinfiore hopped from foot to foot. He had no idea what dragons liked to call themselves.

Sandrino whispered in his ear.

'Silver-Lightning?' said Mandorlinfiore.

'Good choice,' said the dragon, 'but no. Not quite me that one.'

Fabio whispered in his ear.

'Bronze-Heart?' said Mandorlinfiore.

The dragon appeared thoughtful then, as much as a giant fire-breathing flying lizard could, then licked its lips. 'You know,' said the dragon, 'that was my father's name.'

'I see,' said Mandorlinfiore.

'Do you?' said the dragon.

## 40. Gobbled Up?

The dragon craned its long neck forwards and sniffed at Mandorlinfiore. 'I said I would eat you if you did not guess my name,' it said, 'before I do would you like to know what name I chose for myself today?'

'If you are to introduce yourself to me dragon then it would be very poor manners to eat me,' said Mandorlinfiore, 'so no. While death might be an inconvenience and will certainly thwart some of my plans for my loved ones, I will not stand for bad manners.'

'But it's such a pretty name,' said the dragon.

'That may be,' said Mandorlinfiore, 'but a name is only as pretty as it sounds when spoken aloud by a good friend.'

'Oh dear,' said the dragon, 'I fear you might be right.'

'I am right,' said Mandorlinfiore, 'now if you would be so kind either excuse me or eat me. Either way I shall be gone.'

'Did you know my father, Bronze-Heart?' said the dragon. 'I did not, no.' said Mandorlinfiore.

'He was horrid,' said the dragon, 'he insisted I have some dreadful warrior name.'

'For goodness sake dragon,' said Mandorlinfiore, 'bite my head off and crunch up my bones, I am tired of waiting.'

'I'm sorry,' said the dragon, 'I forget myself. It has been such a long time since I had any visitors.' The dragon unfurled its wings and stretched. 'My name is Rosa-Fury.'

'Rosa-Fury,' said Mandorlinfiore, 'is a beautiful name, and you are a beautiful dragon.'

'It sounds so nice when you say it,' said Rosa-Fury, 'I am sorry about the threat to eat you now.'

'Indeed. I would be disappointed if you were to eat me now, Rosa-Fury,' said Mandorlinfiore.

'Do you think,' said Rosa-Fury, 'that we could be friends?'

## 41. A Deal with a Dragon!

Dragons, by and large, it is fair to say, have not been seen in the best light in European legend. While it might be true that a small number of young princesses have been fed to these creatures by despicable rulers, it is not true to say that a dragon cannot survive on any other food.

In fact, most dragons prefer fish or goat and there was tell of a pizza eating dragon too, but that's another story.

Rosa-Fury liked a nice trout or two but had little more than eels and crayfish to eat from the underground stream which ran through her cavern.

'If you let me carry the King's gold back to his strong room, I shall bring you a basket of trout,' said Mandorlinfiore.

'I should like to go outside and stretch my wings,' said Rosa-Fury, 'the cavern is so dreadfully cramped.'

'If you can save my life by returning the gold,' said Mandorlinfiore, 'then I promise I will help you find a way out of here.'

'I do so like gold,' said Rosa-Fury, 'but I do like you too.'

'If I fail to deliver my promise,' said Mandorlinfiore, 'you can suck the gold back out of the strong room.'

The dragon chuckled and blew a little puff of smoke. 'I am a magnet for gold. It cannot help but be drawn to me; for it knows I love it so.'

'Do we have a deal?' said Mandorlinfiore.

'Are we to be friends?' said Rosa-Fury.

'Until I die, through whatever fate sends us, I will remain your friend Rosa-Fury,' said Mandorlinfiore.

'How exciting,' said Rosa-Fury, 'will you read me poetry?'

'Probably not,' said Mandorlinfiore, 'but I may send someone who will.'

'Stand back,' said Rosa-Fury, 'I'm going to put the gold back in your strong room.'

The dragon turned around and slid her tail up the staircase, through the secret passage and into the strong room. She gathered up gold upon her nose and with a shrug and a wriggle sent it spinning along her spine.

*A wide dragon smile.*

## 42. The King's Pardon

'You have a new choice,' said the King of Zonza, 'you may either go free, with your saddlebags of gold, or you become my Chief Treasurer.'

Mandorlinfiore was covered in fish, Rosa-Fury was a messy eater, and he desperately wanted a bath and a comfortable bed.

'You will have a suite of rooms, a man-servant and a chamber-maid,' the King continued, 'all in all you could do worse.'

'I will be your Chief Treasurer your Highness,' said Mandorlinfiore, 'until such time as I need to continue my quest.'

'Then it is settled,' said the King, 'you will not leave Zonza. Few do with their heads still attached.' Then he turned to his guards, 'Execute those thieves and brigands who called themselves accountants. I cannot afford them more lodging in my dungeons.'

'A moment your Royal Highness Sir,' said Mandorlinfiore, 'I would like very much to have two or three people who may have a talent for counting to help me. Before you chop off their heads please allow me to save the best heads for myself.'

'How very sensible,' said the King, 'I knew I made a good choice when I appointed you. Send the rejects to the executioner in the morning.'

'Yes, your Highness,' said Mandorlinfiore.

'Was there anything else?' said the King.

Mandorlinfiore thought of Rosa-Fury curled on a mountain of gold in her cavern beneath the impregnable Castle of Zonza.

'No, your Highness,' said Mandorlinfiore.


## 43. Debates and Decisions

As Mandorlinfiore settled into his new rooms his ghosts became anxious that he might take far too long to settle their business.

'He will grow slow with the comforts of this Castle,' said Escobar, 'remember how he ate all of those pancakes.

What is to stop the royal kitchens from weighing him down?'

'We must keep on at him,' said Sandrino, 'if it wasn't for us, he would never have found the secret passage and would be in the dungeon by now.'

'We didn't help him much with that dragon,' said Fabio.

'True,' said Escobar, 'but we saved his life all the same.'

'That's twice now,' said Sandrino, 'don't forget the fight with the King of the Animals.'

'So first we plot to murder him and now we work hard to save him,' said Fabio, 'and the next thing will be how to get him out of Zonza with his head still on his shoulders.'

* * *

'That man you brought in with all the horses and the treasure chest,' said Belfioré's maid, 'found all the King's missing gold.'

'His eyes are the deepest brown,' said Belfioré.

'He's the Chief Treasurer now,' said the maid.

'Don't you think he has a fine nose?' said Belfioré.

'They say he talks to himself and then stops and listens,' said the maid, 'either it's magic or he's mad.'

'I don't care,' said Belfioré, 'he doesn't seem snooty or vain and full of his own importance. I saw him stop and stroke Hector the cat.'

'Then there must be magic in him,' said the maid, 'That cat would more likely take off your arm than let a man stroke him.'

'He spoke to him too,' said Belfioré, 'and I swear Hector was listening. I have decided I should show him round.'

'Hector knows his way about,' said the maid.

'I didn't mean the cat,' said Belfioré.

## 44. Singing in the Bath

Mandorlinfiore took a long time to wash all of the fish scales out of his hair. His new manservant had to make several journeys with fresh buckets of hot water from the kitchens.

There were bubbles and ointments and shampoos he had never seen before, and so he filled the bath until it splashed over the side. As he scrubbed so he sang.

He sang the old sea shanties he had heard on the quayside as the merchant ships unloaded. He sang the songs he learned from the sailors as they set up their ships to make ready to leave.

*'O pull on the ropes,*
*Pull on the ropes,*
*Heave the sail high men,*
*We'll swagger over the seven seas,*
*Before we kiss your maids again~'*
*'There was a fish called Mary,*
*Whose eyes were very scary,*
*She had a lip, Over which she'd trip,*
*That lovely fish called Mary~'*
*'Olives and wine,*
*Olives and wine,*
*Silver and gold,*
*Silver and gold,*
*Silks all fine,*
*Silks all fine,*
*Make I so bold,*
*Make I so bold~'*

He sang songs from old Egypt and Persia and Athens and was starting a ditty from England about a pretty maid when there was a commotion at the door to his chambers.

'But your Highness I insist!' said his manservant.
'But so do I.'
'Please your Highness.'
'Don't be silly, I have seen a man in a tub before!'
And before Mandorlinfiore had finished the first chorus Belfioré was standing before him.

*'I shall no more go a-wooing,'*

He sang, and then stopped. He was confused. Taught as a young man to stand for a fine lady when she entered the room, or indeed shop, especially for royalty, he started to get up. He then remembered he was in the bath.
At the last minute his manservant arrived with a vast towel which saved his modesty.
'Your Highness,' he said.
'Call me Belfioré,' said the Princess, 'and I shall call you Mandorlinfiore.'
'How can I assist?' said Mandorlinfiore.

## 45. Of Love and All It's Charms

As I believe we have noted already, love can cause all manner of complications in life. For a Princess there are many more difficulties, especially if the man she is in love with is not high born.
For Mandorlinfiore, falling in love was also tricky. He was a man on a quest for the truth of his birth, there was not the time or the convenience for the luxury of love.
But in love he was, from the moment he met Belfioré's gaze, he knew that there could be no other person in the world for him.

Belfioré knew this straight away and realised that there would be no easy way for them to be together.

Even so, there are those who would maintain that love can conquer all, but still others who would say that love is blind. The poets and singers down the ages have attempted many times to tell us what love is like, but really and truly you will only know for certain when it strikes.

And then you will be certain of little else.

Why are we talking about all this you might ask, when there are dragons and ghosts and quests afoot?

Simply because of all enchantments, devices and spells that may be cast on people by the Mazerre, or the Gods of other things, the most powerful, intoxicating charm, lies within us all.

Mandorlinfiore took to writing poetic notes, which Escobar, Sandrino and Fabio tried to catch in the candle flame, or blow out the window, or wet in the bath, to no avail.

Belfioré took to reading his notes and would spend the day a-swooning in her chambers, while the King muttered, and the Queen packed for another trip to the mainland.

And all this time a dragon sniffed and grizzled that she should have had some poetry by now, for the gold she had returned in good faith.

## 46. Strange Goings On

Belfioré's maid was most worried. She had seen her mistress become excited and distracted by many things over the years.

There was the time that Belfioré had decided she would not set another foot upon the ground by climbing into the trees in the Forest of Zonza. The maid, whose name was Maria, was very upset to have to climb to attend to her.

Then there was the time that Belfioré had decided she should live a life of absolute silence. Maria was driven mad muffling doors and tiptoeing around, shushing the dogs and making up sign language.

And we cannot forget the time that Belfioré spent pretending to be the Prince of Tangier in order to win the hand of the King of Zonza's daughter. Herself in other words.

Each time Belfioré went off on an all absorbing tangent Maria had been able to bring her back down to earth by reminding her of her horse.

'Perhaps you should take a ride out?' said Maria, 'It is a beautiful day.'

'He tells me he is the servant of my heart,' said Belfioré.

'I'm certain that a ride upon your white mare will make you feel very jolly,' said Maria.

'He has the chest of a stallion,' said Belfioré.

'He has a treasure chest all right,' said Maria, 'I'd be keen to know what's so special about it.'

'He has turned a key in my heart,' said Belfioré.

There was a knock at the door to the Princess's rooms. It was a messenger from the treasury. He made a little bow, 'Please your Highness, but His Majesty has taken Mandorlinfiore and put him in the dungeon since all of the King's gold has disappeared.'

Belfioré let out a cry of pain, 'No!'

'I am afraid it is true your Highness,' said the messenger, 'and he is to be executed in the morning.'

'Will they hang him?' asked Maria.

'I believe they will ma'am,' said the messenger.

'I don't think so,' said Belfioré, 'take me to the dungeons.'

# 47. The Dungeons of Zonza

Dungeons are not supposed to be pleasant places to spend any time at all, least of all your final hours. For a bandit a dungeon is mortal hell. For a dead bandit it is much the same.

Mandorlinfiore had been stripped of his fine robes and sat quietly on the cold flagstone floor of his cell. The cells were iron cages set in rows on opposite walls.

All of the accountants he had saved before were in the cells across the hall. They stared and muttered and grumbled. Before Mandorlinfiore had rescued them there had been no set date for their hanging. No one had seemed too bothered.

The prisoners might have been able to earn their freedom by fighting in battle for the King, or by working on some difficult and arduous road building in the mountains.

But now the day after tomorrow had been set for their execution. The King of Zonza had ordered a number of new gallows to be constructed and had sent messengers throughout his Kingdom to announce the grand spectacle. In those days, before anyone had invented things like the television or even newspapers, a public execution was both an entertainment and a way of letting everyone know who was in charge.

The King of Zonza was very keen on being seen to be in charge. In the yard outside the dungeon the drummers were practising their drum rolls while the carpenters drummed nails into wood.

Inside the dungeons Mandorlinfiore felt the eyes of his fellow condemned men upon him. Escobar, Sandrino and Fabio paced up and down in his cell.

'Can you not be still?' said Mandorlinfiore.

'We have saved your life many times,' said Escobar, 'but this time I do not see how we can save you, and you will not be able to help us anymore.'

'What will you do?' said Mandorlinfiore.

'We are working out what we must do next, what is best for us, since you had forgotten about us,' said Escobar.

'That may be true,' said Mandorlinfiore, 'and for that I am sorry. I wish you luck, but I am not yet ready to be hanged.'

Escobar sat down and rested his head on his knees. 'At least your bonce will remain attached,' he said.


## 48. A Prison Visit


'I must go to him, but I couldn't bear to see him in chains,' said Belfioré.

'If you wait too long, he'll start to smell,' said Maria, 'they don't give them baths in prison you know.'

Privately Maria was pleased to see the end of another of her Royal Highnesses fads, but a little sad that it would end in a hanging. Still there would be honeyed chestnuts and other delights to make the event more fun.

'I must take him something to sweeten his last days,' said Belfioré.

'Honeyed chestnuts?' said Maria, thinking of the treats a decent hanging brought.

'No Maria, not that, but perhaps I could soothe his soul with a little poetry?' said Belfioré.

Before Maria could think of an objection Belfioré had found her copy of 'Collected Poetry from Ancient Tymes' and was putting on her boots.

In these distant days, books were very rare and precious things which were handmade by craftsmen and artists. Any book in the possession of a Princess was likely to have been very valuable indeed.

'Princess,' said Maria, 'you cannot take a book into the dungeon; it is full of cut throats and thieves.'

'They are all behind bars. I have no fear for my book,' said Belfioré.

'Then I must come with you and make sure those brigands do not try anything!' said Maria.

And so they left the royal chambers and made their way down to the prison yard. The drummers were still drumming, and the carpenters were still hammering and sawing.

At the prison gates the guards stepped aside to let them through. The dungeons did not smell very nice and Maria held her nose. Belfioré ignored the stink and searched out the face of the man she loved.

He was in a cell on his own talking to himself.

'Good morning,' said Belfioré, 'I have come to read you some poetry to make the time pass in a more agreeable way.'

Mandorlinfiore leapt to his feet, 'That's it! That's the answer! Thank you, thank you, thank you,' he said.

Well I never, thought Maria, I never ever saw a man so keen for poetry before!

## 49. Saint George's Dragon

Scholars have sought for centuries the true meaning of the story of Saint George and the Dragon and there have been many attempts to place these events in history.

But it is true to say that no written account exists by any witness and that all we really know is whatever has been remembered and passed on from mother to son or sung by bards and travelling minstrels and mariachis.

Had there been a scribe to hand to record the extraordinary feats ascribed to Saint George then we might find them hard to stomach because, and I can tell you this from a very reliable source, no dragon lost their life by the hand of this knight.

The dragon was still very much alive and lay upon a heap of gold in a cavern beneath the Castle of Zonza. And what do you suppose she thought of our great Saint George, honoured both in Greece and England for her murder?

Not much it would seem. Rosa-Fury had never been one for eating human beings. She rather liked them in fact. She liked their poetry, their music and songs. She also liked spaghetti and meatballs. But none of that seems to fit in a heroic legend does it?

As we all know, Saint George saved a Kingdom and a Princess from the ravages of a terrifying dragon. As Rosa-Fury remembers it a number of burly gold miners had broken into her home and had decided that her hoard was theirs.

They called for a knight to chase her off and one by one they came and one by one they would charge with their heads down and lances raised.

Rosa-Fury was able to dodge the blows and would pick them up and fly across the sea with them, leaving them on strange shores. They were never seen again.

Then one day another knight arrived. This one left horse and lance behind and a sword sheathed but carried an open book. Rosa-Fury feared magic, but instead, heard for the first time the poetry of the ancients.

Every day the knight would read to her while the gold miners carried away her treasure. They could not take the heap she laid upon and so some gold had to remain.

Then there was a loud deafening noise and the cavern was sealed up. Rosa-Fury thought at first that it must have been an accident, but time passed. Centuries passed and no-one came back to read poetry to her again.

## 50. A Condemned Man's Promise

'You must go to the strong room,' said Mandorlinfiore, 'I made a promise to someone who lives beneath it. It is the only way our lives can be saved.'

'If my father hangs you then I will kill myself,' said Belfioré.

'That won't do us any good,' said Mandorlinfiore, 'I know some dead people and they're not happy about it.'

'Is that who you talk to when you are on your own?' said Belfioré.

'Yes,' said Mandorlinfiore, 'is it very obvious?'

'Everyone has noticed it.'

'Then let me introduce you to Escobar, Sandrino and Fabio,' said Mandorlinfiore.

The three mustachio'd bandits bowed to the Princess, although they were invisible to her.

'Pleased to make your acquaintance,' said Belfioré, 'how did you meet them?'

'They tied me to a tree and then killed each other in a squabble as to how to split my gold between them,' said Mandorlinfiore.

'That's not it,' said Escobar.

'You got us all wrong,' said Sandrino.

'I'll not talk to him when he's dead,' said Fabio.

'But they have saved my life on more than one occasion since then,' said Mandorlinfiore, 'and for that I am grateful, because without them I would never have met you.'

Belfioré blushed, as did Maria.

'Now you must go to the strong room and get into the gold room. Hector will help you,' said Mandorlinfiore, 'Tell him I sent you and that he is to show you the secret passage if he wants me to get him any more treats from the fishmonger.'

'You want me to talk to a cat?' said Belfioré.

'Yes,' said Mandorlinfiore, 'if he pretends not to understand then put him in a basket and bring him here to me.'

'Then you must fulfil the promise I made to the creature Rosa-Fury,' said Mandorlinfiore, 'and read her poetry on condition that all of your father's gold is returned in time to save our lives.'

'I will do it,' said Belfioré.


## 51. Hector's Mouse


Belfioré and her maid Maria walked as quickly as they could past the carpenters as they crashed nails into the timbers that would hold the hanging ropes. They tiptoed past the drummers beating out their deadly rhythms. They marched past the braziers where the sellers of honeyed chestnut were preparing their treats.

At the door to the strong room the guards let Belfioré pass. They were not guarding very much more than a few chests of silver and were busy worrying more about their jobs than who they let in.

The gold room echoed. The empty chests lay on their sides. Their lids were broken and on top of one there stood a mouse, eyed from across the room, by a cat.

We are used to seeing mice scuttle and dash on all fours but this one was up on its hind legs with its head tilted right back as if searching for something on the ceiling.

It waved its front paws and then clasped them together as if in prayer.

'Excuse me,' said Belfioré.

The mouse looked straight at her and then did a backward flip and disappeared behind the treasure chest.

'Oh dear,' said Belfioré, 'I didn't mean to scare you.'

'Who are you talking to?' said Maria, 'I don't see anyone.'

'I'm not scared,' came a shrill little voice, 'you made me jump that's all.'

'Oh my,' said Maria, 'a mouse!' And she turned and fled.

'Hee hee, saw the old lady off!' said the mouse.

'What poor manners,' said Belfioré, 'and here you are born and raised in the Castle of Zonza.'

The mouse appeared on top of the chest once more, this time brandishing a two-inch sword. 'I apologise your Highness,' said the mouse, and he bowed, 'but when you are small in a big world it is easy to get over excited when a giant flees.'

'You know who I am,' said Belfioré, 'please introduce yourself.'

'Princess, he is my mouse,' said Hector, who had been napping on the desk. He yawned and stretched and said, 'pay no attention. If he is rude please accept my profound apologies. I will eat him later.'

## 52. A Matter of Scale

If the mouse was a small creature in a big world then it must be true to say that a dragon may be a big creature in a small world.

Should the world become just the right size for a mouse then it would be far too small for us. As you can probably imagine, when Belfioré stood in front of the dragon, she felt very much how the mouse must feel when standing in front of a cat, especially one like Hector.

'Good morning,' said Belfioré, 'I am Belfioré and I have come to read poetry from my book to Rosa-Fury. Please? Is that you?'

Rosa-Fury had been in a bad mood for some time. She felt a little better having emptied the strong room of all its gold, but all of the old bad feelings about being stuck in the cavern had returned.

She began to smile at Belfioré. Now if you have ever met a dragon you will know that it takes a long time for a dragon to smile as they have so many teeth. I would not need to tell you that from start to finish it can take many minutes.

By the time a dragon's smile has reached from one side to another, and all of the razor sharp, diamond hard, teeth are revealed most people will have run away.

But Belfioré stood absolutely still and waited and watched until every last one of Rosa-Fury's teeth were on display. And then the dragon began to laugh. She snorted little puffs of smoke.

Then, abruptly, the smile finished. 'I am not Rosa-Fury anymore,' she said, 'I am Antigone, now read to me.'

'I know that story,' said Belfioré, 'she was the girl in the secret room behind the wall. I see how you must be feeling.'

'Read to me,' said the dragon.

'Of course,' said Belfioré, and she opened her book to page one.

There was a rustling at her shoulder. Hector's mouse had climbed up to her ear. 'I love poetry,' he said.

As she read the old poems Belfioré watched the dragon lose creases and wrinkles as it began to relax. She read and read and was halfway through the book before she knew it.

## 53. A Bankrupt King

The King of Zonza was in a terrible frenzy. He had no gold, so he could have no army. He had no gold, so he could have no ships. He had no gold, so he could have no castle.

He was ruined. The Queen was still away in Florence. If the news got out, he knew she would never return. His only chance was to recover the stolen gold.

He went out on to the battlements and stared down at the preparations in the Prison Yard and realised that the only way he could find out what had happened was if his new treasurer could tell him.

'I will go to the Prison and speak with Mandorlinfiore. If he insists on ruining me then I shall have no option but to ruin him,' said the King, 'I will trade his life for information.'

Now the King was not a pleasant enemy. There had been those who had opposed his wishes and others who had sought to rob him over the years, and he had dealt with them quite wickedly.

While some Kings delighted in hard labour for brigands and bandits the King of Zonza liked to make sure that his prisoners confessed entirely to their misdeeds.

Sometimes this required a little extra persuasion, often with the use of interesting new technologies developed by his carpenters and blacksmiths.

One machine, elegantly called 'The Elucidator', was extremely successful. It worked on the principle that the more light you shone upon something then the clearer the truth became.

The prisoner would be clamped to a frame which in turn had an array of magnifying glasses set above. Each glass could be adjusted so as to focus the rays of the sun on any particular part of the body.

In the clear mountain air of the Castle of Zonza, where the light was pure, it was an efficient device, most of the time. Today, however, the sun was hidden behind thick cloud.

The King would have to use something else. Perhaps the machine called 'The Press' which was an efficient way to squeeze out the truth.

This simple device consisted of two oak slabs with a screw and handle, and a bucket in which to catch the slops.

The King ran through his list of truth-seeking equipment as he made his way to the Prison. When he saw Mandorlinfiore he simply said, 'It is 'The Tank' for you.'

## 54. The Dragon's Saint George

'You know,' said Antigone, 'I feel like calling myself Rosa-Fury again after all those lovely poems.'

'I'm glad I made you happy,' said Belfioré.

'Me too, but I think I shall call myself Goldentail, a name someone guessed recently,' said Goldentail, 'I think his name was Mandorlinfiore. He brought me some lovely fish and promised to read me some poetry.'

'I'm sure he will,' said Belfioré, 'as it was Mandorlinfiore who asked me to come and read to you as he had been too busy.'

'Oh dear,' said Goldentail, 'I'm afraid I got sulky and took all of the gold he was looking after. I suppose I should put it back.'

'That would be nice,' said Belfioré.

'He won't be cross?' said Goldentail, 'George was cross a lot of the time, except when she was reading poetry.'

'I'm sorry,' said Belfioré, 'did you say 'she'?'

'Why yes,' said Goldentail, 'Georgiana was a Princess tired of having to sit and watch all the fun. But when she put armour on she could have been any knight.'

'How did you know she was a Princess,' said Belfioré, 'if her disguise was so good?'

'Well we talked,' said Goldentail, 'she would read the poems, just like you did. In fact, when I closed my eyes it could have been Princess Georgiana in your place.'

'You mean Saint George?' said Belfioré.

'Saint George you say,' said Goldentail, 'well I never heard that before. My, didn't she do well for herself?'

'The songs and stories I have heard tell of how Saint George rescues a Princess from a Dragon.' said Belfioré.

'She always seemed ambitious,' said Goldentail, 'last thing I heard, she had met a Mazerre by the name of Merlin. Then my cavern was sealed by magic.'

'That must have been difficult,' said Belfioré.

'My dear,' said Goldentail, 'magic does not last forever. Time wears it away as it wears away everything.'

## 55. The Tank

There are many ways to find out the truth. One is to simply ask as many people as possible who might know something and then put the various pieces of information together.

Another is to make use of a truth potion, which is usually distilled from various fruits or vegetables, but this can often make for exaggeration.

Yet another is to use the threat of a diminished quality of life, or torture. The King of Zonza was very pleased with his truth-seeking devices and had yet to meet a liar who could not be reformed.

The 'Tank' was a very simple machine, which the King was very proud of. It put together some of his most effective truth extracting techniques.

First the 'liar' is strapped into a harness. Then this person is suspended in the air over a great iron tank full of water. In the water are a good number of hungry fish.

The 'liar' is first raised above this tank and then lowered until completely covered by water. The dippings continue until the 'liar' consents to reform and tell the truth or is eaten by the hungry fish.

The fish in the tank are not sharks or any other savage hunter, that sort of thing is impossible to get hold of in the wild mountainous Kingdom of Zonza. Instead they are small local fish.

Their curiosity, however, is often mistaken for hunger, and so their nibbling is taken for worse than it really is. But added to the threat of drowning, it makes for an efficient truth-seeking device.

Mandorlinfiore had been raised by the sea and had spent many summers full of happy days playing in the water with his brother and could hold his breath for a good number of minutes. There were always lots of fish in the sea too, so the 'Tank' held no fear for him.

The King of Zonza gave the command and Mandorlinfiore was raised up to the rafters on the ropes.

'Are you going to tell me what you have done with all of my gold?' said the King.

Mandorlinfiore said nothing.

'I hate to do this to anyone,' said the King, 'especially to one who showed so much promise as a treasurer. The counting house book has never looked so good.'

Mandorlinfiore still said nothing.

'Perhaps my fish will loosen your tongue?' said the King, and he motioned to the guards to lower Mandorlinfiore into the 'Tank'.

*The endless forest.*

## 56. A Fortune Restored

It did not take long for Goldentail the Dragon to send all of the gold she had taken back to the strong room in the counting house.

'I really am too headstrong,' said Goldentail, 'I wish there was some way out of here so I could fly and stretch my wings, that might put me back on a more even keel.'

'I'll see what I can do,' said Belfioré, 'but I dare not promise anything in case there's nothing I can do.'

'Do not worry,' said Goldentail, 'the magic is wearing away every day, and I am really quite a patient dragon.'

'Saint George has been gone a long, long time,' said Belfioré.

'Yes,' said Goldentail, 'but I know that old Mazerre is still around somewhere.'

'Will you try and find the Mazerre when you escape the cavern?' said Belfioré.

'I really don't think I could be bothered with all the trouble my dear,' said Goldentail.

'But now I must go and make sure Mandorlinfiore is set free,' said Belfioré, 'I will return soon.'

Belfioré turned to leave. At the foot of the steps that rose through the secret passage to the strong room sat both Hector and his mouse.

'That was a rather lovely reading,' said Hector, 'I must ensure that I attend the next.'

'I didn't understand a word of it,' said the mouse, 'but it sounded very nice.'

'Thank you both,' said Belfioré, 'now I must hurry to the Prison and save my dear Mandorlinfiore.'

She hurried up the stairs and into the strong room where she had to climb over chests of gold that were stacked up to the ceiling.

She ran past the carpenters putting finishing touches to their fine new gallows.

She ran past the drummers who were now polishing their drums.

She ran through the Prison doors to find Mandorlinfiore's cell was empty.

'Where is he?' Belfioré demanded of the guards.

'He is telling the truth with the King,' said the guard, 'and I think he may be in 'The Tank'.'

Belfioré had many rows with her father, the King of Zonza, over many things, but no row could ever be any fiercer than the arguments they had had over her father's 'Machines of Truth'.

The King had many reasons for keeping and developing them. Belfioré had as many reasons for taking them to bits. The Queen reminded Belfioré that every fine house in Europe maintained such devices and it was not up to the Zonzas to be different.

'Just because everyone else is doing it,' said Belfioré, 'does not mean that it is right.'

'Take them to bits when you are Queen,' said the King of Zonza, 'and see how long you last.'

## 57. Underwater Life

As I think has been noted before, Mandorlinfiore was keen on swimming in the sea as a boy and was competitive in breath holding competitions with his brother. Once on the bottom of 'The Tank' he was amused to find Escobar, Sandrino and Fabio in there with him.

'The girl is reading to the Dragon,' said Escobar, 'and the Dragon is calling herself Goldentail now.'

'The gold will soon be returned, and you will be pardoned again,' said Sandrino.

'Then you must escape from this awful place,' said Fabio, 'and never come back.'

'Oh dear Fabio,' said Escobar, 'I do not like the look he just gave you. I fear our man is in love with the King's daughter and may not be able to flee.'

'Then we will remain and wait,' said Sandrino, 'and watch as he grows old.'

'How will we manage to wait,' said Fabio, 'when our dear ones starve without our legacies.'

'I know not,' said Escobar, 'but Mandorlinfiore is a good man and he will do what he thinks is best. He would not let our children go without shoes.'

Mandorlinfiore nodded to let the three mustachio'd bandits know that he could hear and understand them. He was beginning to feel light-headed as he began to need to take another breath.

The King waved to his guards to pull him up again. Mandorlinfiore surfaced and drew in a huge lungful of air. 'Are you ready to tell me where all my gold is?' said the King.

Mandorlinfiore shook his head.

'Down,' said the King.

Mandorlinfiore was lowered again.

'Where did you go?' said Fabio, 'only joking. No. Really, you must not get yourself killed.'

'Fabio is right,' said Sandrino, 'This is no way to go on since we worked so hard to keep you in one piece.'

'Leave him be,' said Escobar, 'let us check on the gold.'

At the bottom of 'The Tank' there was a drain. It let the fish out into the Royal fishponds and meant that it could be kept clean between dippings. It is not particularly obvious to the naked, submerged eye, but Mandorlinfiore spotted it as the three mustachio'd bandits walked away.

The rope used to tie him had swollen in the water and as the knots were poorly tied by guards who had never been sailors, because as everyone knows, sailors always know the very best knots to use, Mandorlinfiore slipped his bonds and swam down to the drain.

He pulled it up with both hands and set the cover to the side. The water instantly began pouring through it. With it went Mandorlinfiore.

## 58. An Angry Princess

'Father,' said Belfioré, 'I have no idea why you might bring Mandorlinfiore, your Treasurer, here when your counting house is stacked to the ceiling with gold.'

'What?' said the King, 'Are you sure?'

'Of course, I'm sure,' said Belfioré, 'I have just come from there. It looks very nice for being cleaned.'

'Cleaned?' said the King, 'You mean to say that I am not bankrupt?'

'That's right,' said Belfioré. She looked around the room looking for Mandorlinfiore. 'Your new man has done a very good job.'

'But what will I do with all those nice new gallows?' said the King, 'I can't let them go to waste.'

'What have you done with him?' said Belfioré, 'Where is Mandorlinfiore?'

'I really don't know,' said the King, 'one minute he was inspecting the workings of my machines and the next he was gone.'

'You weren't torturing him for stealing all of your gold?' said Belfioré.

'No, well yes,' said the King, 'maybe a little bit, but he said he liked to swim.'

'You dipped him didn't you,' said Belfioré, 'I wish I could burn all of your awful machines.'

'He was very good at holding his breath,' said the King, 'but now he has disappeared, along with all of the water. Have you any idea how long it takes to fill 'The Tank'?'

'If I don't find him,' said Belfioré, 'you can be sure of one thing.'

'What's that?' said the King.

'There won't be a speck of gold left in this castle.' Belfioré turned on her heel and ran across the yard to the stables. She saddled her horse and rode up to the prison doors.

'Jailor,' said Belfioré, 'you must set the accountants free. They have work to do in the counting house. Tell the King it is my command. They need to count all of the gold in the strong room.'

She rode up to the gallows where the carpenters had begun knotting ropes.

'Carpenters,' said Belfioré, 'you are to take these gallows and turn them into a stage for minstrels and other entertainers. There will be no executions tomorrow. Tell the King it is my command.'

Then she turned her horse to the Western gate and galloped out of the castle and on to the path that led to the royal ponds.

## 59. The Lives of the Dead

Now it might be supposed that where once many people lived, many people also died. So, it is not unreasonable to imagine that there might be a number of those who still hang on to unfinished business.

Certainly, when our three mustachio'd bandits arrived at the Castle of Zonza in the City of Zonza there seemed to be quite a number of dead people about the place.

In a location as old as Zonza some of the ghosts had been dead for some time. If you have ever been dead yourself you will know this, but most of us have not experienced this and will probably not for some time to come.

Escobar was expecting there to be a good number of the dead in Zonza and he set about talking to them and asking questions. Most would stand about awaiting a rescue, but there were one or two with purpose.

There was Bezan, an old bandit, so unusually old he had a white beard, who had been waiting two hundred years for someone to find his bones and put them in a cemetery.

Then there was Reeta, a merchant from Sardinia with a key hidden away that needed to be discovered.

And there was an old woman who would not give her name but would just ask to hear poetry.

There were none who could help Escobar and his companions discover where Mandorlinfiore might have ended up, and so they began to fear the worst.

If he did not turn up soon then they may have to remain amongst the dead for all time. Sandrino and Fabio took this news badly and decided to haunt the King, but they had little effect on him.

Escobar resolved to find Mandorlinfiore if he could and started in 'The Tank' by following the drain.

## 60. The Underground River

As a boy, Mandorlinfiore and his brother Mandorlinfiore had had many diving and holding-your-breath competitions in the sea at Solenzara. This was a very good thing as he didn't get a chance for another breath for a record-breaking time.

Just when he thought he was sure to drown he surfaced in a low roofed cavern. The water flowed slowly and was icy cold. He gulped a great lung-full of air.

He put his arms out in front and began to swim with the flow of the water.

Now if you have ever been deep under the ground, in a cave, or a mine, or perhaps your house has a cellar, then you will know that it can be extremely dark. It can be darker than night-time as there are no stars, darker than just closing your eyes.

In this underground river there was no light at all. Mandorlinfiore might as well be blind. There could have been a waterfall ahead, or sharp rocks, there was no way he could tell.

All he could do was hope for the best as the current pulled him on. The river turned and twisted through the mountain. Mandorlinfiore was rushed past stone worn smooth by centuries of whooshing water.

His clothes tore, his shoes were lost, but he still had hope. Then suddenly he was propelled into the light and, for a moment, it seemed like he was flying.

He blinked his eyes to get used to the light and then saw that he might indeed be flying as he had emerged at the head of a waterfall. The river had spat him out high above a deep blue lake that glittered in the afternoon sun.

Mandorlinfiore had just enough time to turn into a dive as he began falling.


## 61. The King's New Hoard


Many people, to keep things safe, end up putting them under their pillows or beneath the bed, in case anyone should come and try to take away whatever precious thing it is.

The King of Zonza vowed that he would know where all of his gold was all of the time and so he gave orders that the accountants, and the guards, move all of his gold up into his rooms in the great Tower of Zonza.

That way he could sleep with his gold, have breakfast with his gold, and count his gold all day long, if he so wished.

It took quite some time to move, because gold is very heavy, but the King was happy for it to take all year if necessary. The accountants were happy to be out of jail, and the old Treasurer was pleased to have his job back.

No-one spoke of Mandorlinfiore. No-one expected to ever see him again. Few came out of the Machines of Truth room in one piece and it was considered bad luck to talk about them.

By the end of the first week the King's bedchamber had been stacked to the ceiling with chests full of gold. To get to the bed there was a narrow corridor through which only one person at a time could pass.

The bedroom window was blocked so it was also dreadfully dark. Underfoot the floor creaked under the strain of so much weight.

The hallway outside his room was also crowded with chests full of gold and gold bars were stacked to the ceiling. The Queen's bedroom had been left alone. The King knew that to have filled her room too would have caused him far too much trouble.

Time passed and even though the accountants had been labouring for weeks to move the gold, still the strong room did not appear to be getting any less full. But as any accountant will tell you, the more money there is to count the more work they will have to do.

The King ordered that the guest chambers be stacked with his gold, that the throne room be filled and that his library be cleared.

And so it was that before very long the entire Castle of Zonza was stacked from the ground floor, to the rafters of the royal observatory. And still the strong room appeared as full as it ever had been.

'I am the richest King that Zonza has ever seen,' the King declared, 'perhaps I should increase my land and make of

Corsica one Kingdom. Then Spain might take notice and France too.'

And so, he spent some time studying his maps, and outlining lands he took a fancy to with red ink. 'Perhaps I could buy Sardinia?' said the King.

## 62. That Sinking Feeling

As we have discussed before now, time is an interesting idea. Try as we might to count it the way we tally gold, or sheep, or friends, it will always appear to play tricks. Time has the upper hand, it is neither slave nor master, rather we employ machines, clocks of many kinds, which we either worship or despise.

While the King of Zonza was occupied with piling up his hoard, Mandorlinfiore was busy trying to work out where he had ended up. Carried by the current and supported by schools of Corsican fishes, he had whizzed through the Southern Gorge and slipped un-noticed beneath the branches of the Forest of the Werewolves. He had safely manoeuvred through the Razor Rapids but was now stuck on Quicksand Beach.

'How will you get back to Zonza from here?' said Escobar, who had finally caught up with him, 'You have no horse, map or compass, and you are sinking fast.'

'So I am Escobar,' said Mandorlinfiore, 'I think it is about time.'

'Time for what?' said Escobar.

'Time for you to stop asking so many questions,' said Mandorlinfiore, 'You have helped me so much, and I know I have been slow to settle your business, and I am sorry for that.'

'You are in the quicksand up to your knees,' said Escobar.

'But my quest remains, and there are many promises I am still to keep,' said Mandorlinfiore.

'You are in it up to your waist,' said Escobar.

'Up to my neck at least,' said Mandorlinfiore.

'You will be in a minute,' said Escobar.

Then, as the sand rose around his chest Mandorlinfiore closed his eyes, raised his arms above his head and clapped three times, 'Salamanca! Salamanca!' he said.


## 63. On Justice


If you have ever, now wait a minute, what is this? We have all, by the very fact of having lived to an age where a story such as this can be heard, read and enjoyed, and so, assuming that you are at least familiar with all your gifts and that you have known other people, it would be reasonable to expect that you have experienced some one or other situation to have been unfair?

Perhaps you were able to sort things out? Maybe it still sits heavy on your heart as there seems to be nothing you can do to make it better?

Some of you might want to start or join a campaign to improve things or write a letter to a government department. This is all very worthy and is to be expected.

However, justice is sometimes delivered in an unexpected way, and the end result, and how it is arrived at, may be utterly different from what you might have thought should happen in the first place. This is not necessarily a bad thing. It may simply be because those who study law and judgement, if they have a deep understanding of the subject, will have a broader view of the situation than we may be allowed, if we are sitting at the center of the storm.

*The green way.*

## 64. Night Sounds

Rosa-Fury was a very happy giant fire-breathing flying lizard once again. She had re-named herself after Belfioré left and had been allowing herself to feel hopeful.

In the mountains the air is thinner and so sound travels a lot further. Church bells can be heard from one mountain top to another, and goat-herders always know where their goats are. In the same way small sounds can echo for miles underground. If you add to this the sensitivity of a dragon's hearing, then you might be able to imagine Rosa-Fury's surprise when she heard the first cicada.

It was just a little chirrup to start with, but then she could hear more and more, until it was all she could hear. She blew a little flame and then climbed down from her hoard of gold. The night chorus grew louder as she made her way down stream, toward the ancient entrance to her cavern. After perhaps a half mile of underground waterfalls, pools and chasms that she had not seen for an awfully long time, she saw moonlight, and an opening in the rock just large enough for her to squeeze through.

She stood upon a rocky outcrop surrounded by pine forest. All of the cicadas in Corsica must have been at that spot for a party as their singing was deafening.

Rosa-Fury stretched her neck, her legs, her tail, then unfurled her wings.

'I think,' she said, 'I'll just go the once around the island.'

Then she flapped her wings and leapt into the night sky.

## 65. The Call of the Sea

Belfioré had ridden for days non-stop, past the royal ponds and down through the Southern Gorge to the very edge of the Kingdom of Zonza. She contemplated the Forest of the Werewolves and had decided to skirt its borders to the West, riding high through villages so remote no-one had thought to give them a name.

In one such village all of the people spoke in dog language, barking at each other across the village square. In another the people spoke in bird language, whistling and tootling enough to drive anyone completely mad.

At last, when her horse was finally exhausted from chasing up and down mountains for days on end, Belfioré saw the sea. For all of her adventuring nature Belfioré had never been drawn to visit the sea. She had read poems, heard songs, shanties and ballads and even admired paintings, but had her interest quashed by the Queen's insistence that she sail to Florence on the one hand, and the King's contempt for over-seas travel on the other.

Now, as the sun set below the waters of the Mediterranean, and the waves shone pink and silver, she made a decision.

'Tomorrow I will ride down to the sea,' said Belfioré, 'perhaps it is time for me to leave Zonza for a while and seek my own fortune?'

At the next village all of the people spoke in horse language, so she let her white mare negotiate a good rate for a pleasant room at the local inn. Thankfully it was not run by an old God with a number of ancient scores to settle.

Once she had finished a supper of porridge oats, she was able to sleep soundly on a bed of lavender hay.

*A perilous coastline.*

## 66. An Abandoned Hoard

Fabio and Sandrino may have been young and headstrong bandits when they were alive, and now they were dead, nothing much had changed. They were still lured by the glow of gold and had watched as the accountants and the Treasurer continued to move the gold out of the strong room, which kept re-filling overnight. Fabio and Sandrino slipped through the stone wall and down the secret passage into Rosa-Fury's cavern. They saw at once that the dragon was not there.

'Just look at that pile of treasure,' said Fabio.

'It would buy the French and the Spanish Crowns,' said Sandrino.

'And mop up Rome and Venezia too,' said Fabio.

'What about England?' said Sandrino.

'No-one wants to go there,' said Fabio, 'too cold.'

Then something caught Sandrino's eye. 'What's that up there? On top of the pile of gold. The glowy thing?'

'What? Where?' said Fabio.

'Up. Look up,' said Sandrino, and he began to climb the mountain of gold and treasure. Then Fabio let out a gasp as he spotted what his compatriot had seen.

It must be said, that since their poisoning, demise, and internment, life, if we can call it that, had become far more interesting for our bandits. Gone were the tiresome chores of hunting and cooking, murder and robbery, carousing and merrymaking. In their place had come the knowledge of many things we think of as either mythical or merely impossible.

This was one of those things, for atop the dragon's hoard there was an egg. It was twice as high as a full-grown person and glowed with a golden light. Silver markings ran around it like a string of ancient hieroglyphs and, as Fabio and Sandrino came closer, a crack appeared at the top, which spread all the way to the bottom.


## 67. Of News


These days news travels fast, really fast. And if it doesn't travel fast enough it gets made up until the facts can catch up. In the days of our story a lot of news couldn't be reported until someone had set it to a decent tune, made the words rhyme so they were memorable and could be sung. If the tune was a good one the news would travel further. If you could dance or clap along then chances were that the English would eventually learn of the goings on in Corsica.

It was in this way that the story of the battle with the King of the Animals was spread, and also how the Merchant of Solenzara and his wife came to hear how their adoptive son had managed to stem the leak from the King of Zonza's strong room. The old couple were proud to hear the song sung on the quayside, or in the inn, or in the town square at night.

'That's our boy,' said the Merchant to his wife, 'he knows his books.'

'Perhaps we should visit?' said his wife.

It was widely agreed that the road to Zonza must be a much safer journey without the King of the Animals snaring hungry travellers.

'Perhaps we should send Sylvan?' said the Merchant, 'Maybe they would be in need of a good warehouse in the royal city?'

So, the next morning they spoke to Sylvan who readied a pair of carts at once with the finest carpets and silks, embroidered cloths, soaps and unguents, and set off with four men-at-arms to Zonza. He was keen to see his brother again but also proud to be given charge of such an important mission.

He sent a handsome minstrel ahead on a fast horse to let the people of the city know that they would soon be as fit to see, and smell, as the Florentines and Romans across the Tyrrhenian Sea.


## 68. Of Cats and Their Maids


Maria made up Belfioré's bed. She had cleaned all of her clothes and tidied her chambers so that they looked like new. She was used to the Princess staying out for a night or two, but now, after three nights and no sign, she did allow herself to worry a little.

This time it felt different. This time she was not having to cover up for Belfioré as everyone had heard of her row with the King, and so many people had seen her ride out of the city.

Even Hector the cat had changed his mind. When in doubt Hector would always be reassuring. This time though he had simply thought, 'The King's gold will be gathering dust before he sees his daughter again.'

As it was, Maria made herself a promise that no dust would ever be allowed to settle at all in her Lady's chambers, and that none of Hector's fur should ever be allowed to collect anywhere.

Hector meanwhile took his mouse back to the empty strong room where they slipped though the secret door to the cavern. Hector had half a mind to befriend Rosa-Fury, but when he arrived at the foot of the dragon's hoard, he was met with quite an extraordinary scene.

## 69. On The Water

Listening to a story, or reading a tale as long as this one, with as much going on as there is, requires a person to have a pretty good memory for people and things. Some of you will definitely have a better memory than the teller of this tale, who might well have forgotten more things of importance than they dare think about.

But if you can think back to the beginning of our story, or at least to chapter two, you may remember the young fisherman and his wife and the baby boy they had together. Well, since we last heard of them, they went on to have six more sons and seven daughters. The couple's friends said they had enough children to start a town of their own. Indeed, their cottage was so crowded that the father slept in his boats with three of his sons and four of his daughters, all of whom were expert mariners.

They too had heard the songs celebrating the restoration of the King of Zonza's fortune, and the songs telling of the Count of Bonifacio's begging letters. The fisherman and his wife listened out for word of the King's son with a heavy heart, but never was such a one mentioned, although a lovely-but-untamed Princess was regularly sung about.

The fisherman was out on the Tyrrhenian Sea one evening just as it was getting dark, with his boys and girls in their boats, humming the new songs. As they cast their nets the light changed as if a storm was about to race across the straits from Sardinia, but the sea was calm and there was no tell-tale breeze. Fishing is dependent on the weather, so the fisherman tried to read the skies. The sun was gone, but great patches of stars disappeared behind an enormous black shape, and then reappeared again.

Then Abel, the oldest boy said, 'Did you see that huge bat fly past?'

The fisherman said nothing but began to work out how quickly they could make it back to harbour.

Abel's sister, Beulah, said, 'You are mistaken brother, it was a seagull.'

The fisherman held his counsel but began to urgently take in the nets.

Abel and Beulah's brother, Carlo, said, 'It was only a butterfly, blown out to sea.'

The fisherman kept his peace but caught Abel's eye and signalled for him to start rowing for home.

Abel and Beulah and Carlo's sister, Diana, said, 'No. You are all wrong. It was not a bat, or a seagull, neither was it a butterfly. My brothers and sisters, that creature was a dragon.'

There was silence then on the boats, and for a long moment nobody said anything at all.

*Old stones stay silent.*

## 70. Fireworks

So one night you might find yourself sitting out with friends or family, or both, and listening to the song of the cicadas as they sit out with their friends or family in the pine trees which surround you, and you will hear fireworks. You will think, 'My goodness, I am missing some amazing display!' But of course, you will be right. Perhaps you were not in town when the tickets were advertised for sale, or maybe you only just arrived and had no idea? Either way, you make a note and be sure to get a ticket next time, before you forget all about it.

But what if, one night, this same night, a firework goes wrong? What if its holder tilts at an awkward angle and suddenly the pine trees above your head explode in flame and the cicadas are hushed? What then?

Then you run in all directions to escape the flames, while one brave soul takes a fire extinguisher, and another brave soul dashes onto open ground to see what else might come.

And they say, 'That was a dragon!'

Now imagine the silence that statement would cause.

***

Into that gap we can pause a moment to catch our breath and see where we are with the story. The last part of the book is coming up and memory can play tricks with us. It's okay, don't worry, we are still not quite three quarters of the way through yet.

Belfioré is waking up in a town where everyone talks in horse language, to find her white mare is to marry the Mayor.

The King of Zonza is busy paying masons to shore up his tower. All that gold is terribly heavy.

The Queen of Zonza is shopping for soap in Florence, again.

Sylvan, Mandorlinfiore's adoptive brother, has found a marvellous premises just inside the gates to the City of Zonza.

Escobar is sitting by the sea humming a lament.

Fabio and Sandrino are counting themselves lucky to be dead as they watch a dragon's egg slowly hatch.

112

Hector and his mouse have fled and are resting on Maria's lap.

A Moor is leading a huge white ox along a harbour wall and asking after the health of a fisherman's eldest son.

The fisherman's wife is busy mending her slippers, while her husband hums old half-remembered tunes.

Rosa-Fury is sunbathing at the top of Zonza's highest peak, listening to the White Hart recite the poetry of the Dryads.

## 71. Circus! Circus!

If you have been lucky enough to have visited a circus then you will know exactly what to expect, bright lights, bright colours, loud music, applause and laughter.

Most of us do not live on small islands in the Mediterranean Sea and so we may be more used to seeing large convoys of carts, trucks or trains. In the port of Bonifacio, we see instead a small collection of brightly painted fishing boats, with each sail a billboard promising the finest entertainment ever to have docked.

As twilight approaches the fire-eater begins to blow great plumes of flame into the sky. This draws in the early crowd for the clowns to work on, while the band strike up a merry tune. Pretty girls and handsome boys sell trinkets to open-mouthed children, taking coins from their parents.

And then a peculiar sound will rise from one of the boats. A cry, or a growl, or a whoop, and the crowd will change as smaller children cower and older children press forward. Was it a gurgle or a gasp that came from the boat? Then another growl, like the feral cat which lives in the rafters of your hut. What's that? Don't you live in a rough cottage by the docks? Ah, no. Of course not. But if you did, then you might hear it too.

The fire-eater answers each noise with a blast of bright orange flame shot high into the evening sky. The crowd watches as the flames ascend, craning their necks. And then there is an answering plume of flame, as high as the stars. The crowd gasps, and people mutter in awe and ask, 'how does he do that?'

The Moor and his ox do not look out of place on the quayside. They could be a part of the Circus troupe. But the Moor has a faraway look in his eye as he contemplates the crowd of spectators.

## 72. Good Morning

Mandorlinfiore awoke slowly from a strange and confused dream all about dragons and ghosts and talking cats. He snuggled down under his silk sheets and feebly pushed away his own wakefulness. It was no good, the birdsong was particularly loud and there was something kneading his belly.

'Good morning sir,' said Hector.

'What?' said Mandorlinfiore.

'Nice to have you back,' said Hector.

'What?' said Mandorlinfiore.

'Although you appear to have left your manners somewhere else,' said Hector.

'Pardon me?' said Mandorlinfiore.

'Pardon granted,' said Hector, 'now tell me, have you seen the Princess?'

'The Princess?' said Mandorlinfiore.

'Must I repeat everything I say to you?' said Hector, 'The Princess has been missing, as have you. You have been returned to us, so far the Princess has not.'

'Where am I?' said Mandorlinfiore.

'You are in the Castle of Zonza of course,' said Hector, 'and obviously not well in the head.'

'Obviously,' said Mandorlinfiore, 'and feeling worse by the minute.'

'I shall send for your man-servant,' said Hector. He left off kneading the bedclothes, jumped off the bed, and trotted out through the bedroom door.

The manservant quickly decided that Mandorlinfiore was not well and gave him extra blankets and a hot water bottle. Mandorlinfiore soon broke into a sweat and felt quite hot and feverish.

The King of Zonza arrived, anxious that his best accountant should get better as soon as possible and perhaps aid the return of his daughter. He had completely forgotten about losing him in 'The Tank'. As he sat next to the bed, watching the man-servant mop Mandorlifiore's brow, he spotted a long scar on his neck.

'How did you come by that scar young man?' said the King of Zonza, 'It looks like a cut that would nearly kill a man.'

And so Mandorlinfiore told the King of Zonza of how his adoptive father, the Merchant of Solenzara, had discovered him in an almond grove all those years ago.


## 73. A Visit to the Count of Bonifacio


Above the harbour, in his palazzo in the Citadel, the Count of Bonifacio is sweating over his accounts. With all of the improvements and maintenance works he has had to pay for with regard to the Port, he is finding it hard to meet the ever-increasing tax demands from the King of Zonza. The Count has always looked after things at Bonifacio, much as his father, and his father before him. The Port had prospered for centuries. But now, times were hard. The King asked for more every year, while, it has to be admitted, the Port buildings, the jetties, the lighthouse, the cottages, were all aging, and the less gold the Count had to pay for the upkeep, the tattier things became.

As you might well imagine, the songs that reached the citadel of the King's fortune only made the Count sweat the harder for fear of ever more demands on his purse. So, when word came that the King's daughter, the Princess Belfioré, was at his gate, all at once he began to wail. It took an hour for his manservant to calm him enough to face his unexpected guest.

'Your Highness,' he said.

'Count,' said Belfioré, 'I should like to stay under your roof for a little while if I may?'

'Of course, your Highness,' said the Count, bowing low, 'but I am surprised that you travel alone and with no horse?'

'This is not an official visit Count,' said Belfioré, 'and I would be pleased if my Father were not to know I was here for the time being.'

'As you wish Milady,' said the Count.

'And call me Belfioré,' said Belfioré.

'But,' started the Count, 'Belfioré? As you wish.'

'I have decided to travel,' said Belfioré.

'To where?' said the Count.

'I don't know,' said Belfioré, 'but I expect I'll know when I get there.'

She left the Count scratching his head and went for a walk along the Citadel walls. She could see the fire eater below in the harbour. His flame lit up the sails of the circus boats, it flickered across the lightly rippling water and threw enormous dark shadows up the steep cliffs.

A white ox caught her eye. It reminded Belfioré of her white mare, recently married. Next to the ox was a Moor, and he was staring up at the Citadel walls. He seemed to be looking directly at the Princess.

*Narrow streets of old Bonifacio.*

## 74. On the Family Habits of Dragons

Much knowledge of dragons has been lost down the ages. There are few folks around these days with any first-hand experience, and so we have to rely on what has been handed down to us from the old stories.

A lot of what we read, and hear, tends to focus on fully grown beasts, those that fly about terrorizing Kings, Queens, beautiful Princesses and metal armoured knights. There is little to be found in all the libraries concerning the family habits of dragons.

It has been assumed by some that because of their love of gold, and solitary nature, that they must surely be unsuited to a family life. The mistake is to expect dragons to be the same as humans. It is true, that in the long and extravagant histories of dragons that remain to us, a family, or perhaps a flight, or indeed a squadron of dragons is a rare thing, but this should not lead us to believe it impossible.

In truth, we hear of trouble, and it is nearly always trouble, with single dragons simply because their finer instincts are to protect their offspring hiding deep underground, enabling them to make their escape. This is a fine strategy which has helped to preserve generations of dragons to this very day.

Dragons are efficient creatures and extraordinarily long lived, for the most part, including all of those famous and brief encounters with knights, most of which didn't go the way the knight would have you believe. Had your good knight gone up against an angry dragon then it was most likely that he would have been welded tight into his armour before being roasted.

Rosa-Fury had been snuggling up to her egg for quite some time, perhaps for the last ninety-nine years. It was hard to say exactly how long when incarcerated in a cavern deep underground, when the only measure of the passing of time is the slow rhythm of ones' own heartbeat. Now she felt the tug in her heart and knew that the time had come at last for her little one to emerge from his egg.

'What will he be called?' thought Rosa-Fury. It was, as we have already learned, a serious business to name a dragon. It will not do to call a baby dragon Baba de Camelo, even if he is as sweet as roasted almonds. At the same time, even if your baby dragon has a lovely squishy pink tummy, and squeaks every time you tickle it, you must remember that these creatures must be treated with the deepest, and most sober respect.

'He will have a nature name, not a war name,' said Rosa-Fury. 'Maybe something that will make us both think of mountains?'

She flew swiftly and in silence over the mountain tops of Zonza until she spied the entrance to the cavern, whereupon she swooped down and disappeared from view.

## 75. The King of Zonza's Dilemma

The King could not believe his ears. How could this man, lying before him, have been the new-born baby he had taken and abandoned all those years ago? He had been certain that the pigs would have tidied him up in a few quick gulps. Was it true that he was to become a King at last? Then the coin fell into place. The name of this man was Mandorlinfiore. It was obvious. He had been named for the place he had been discovered by that meddling merchant from Solenzara.

And now there was word that another merchant, also from Solenzara, had arrived in Zonza to excite the townsfolk with his exotic carpets and cloths. It was surely a plot. He would have to drive them both out, but in a clever way, so as not to make it seem they were being expelled. The King had never been short on cunning and was well versed in getting what he wanted by stealth, if circumstances required.

He paced the halls of the Castle, between the creaking stacks of gold. He could not bear the thought that his wealth could be taken away by the sickly accountant he had grown to admire. There was a man in Bonifacio who owed him a favour or two, not to mention back taxes. The King of Zonza began a smile that took about an hour to become visible, two more before he bared his teeth, and it was almost dinner time when he was able to let out a tiny chuckle.

He had a plan. And it was perfect.

The cherry on top arrived with a messenger from Bonifacio with an urgent, top secret request for ransom.

## 76. A Royal Plot

The King was not a betting man. He always favoured a sure thing. To hold on to a Kingdom in those days was subject to a certain amount of risk as there were threats on all sides. The King had had the support of a Mazerre at the beginning, but more and more had to rely on alliances, shows of strength and crafty plotting.

So when the King pronounced to Mandorlinfiore that he must go with all speed with his brother to meet the Queen and her daughter at the Citadel of the Count of Bonifacio our hero suspected some sort of trade deal was afoot.

It was. The trade was a life for a life. Upon Belfioré's release Mandorlinfiore would see the insides of the Count's dungeon. The King had doubled the ransom, to be carried on the merchant's wagon, to ensure the Count's enthusiastic compliance. The job the King had started on Mandorlinfiore's neck with a sword, would be completed in Bonifacio with an axe.

It was a happy reunion for Mandorlinfiore and Sylvan. They had not seen each other in a long time and welcomed this opportunity. They had no idea of the King's plot of course.

'How is the new warehouse in Zonza?' said Mandorlinfiore.

'It looks the part,' said Sylvan, 'but there is little real trade here so far. Zonza sounds so much bigger in songs.'

'How are our parents?' said Mandorlinfiore.

'Proud of you brother,' said Sylvan, 'we must visit them on our return.'

The two of them set off early the next morning. The letter for the Count bore the King's seal and was bound within a silk wallet, tied within a leather pouch, locked within a small wooden chest. The King had taken no chances. His instructions were clear. He waved off his accountant satisfied that he would never be seen in Zonza again. And do you know what? The funny thing is, he never was.

# 77. Dragon Songs

It has long been known that sound travels a long way over water, and through thin mountain air. Conversations can take place between fishermen so far apart that they may be invisible over the curve of the world, and debates can range from mountain top to mountain top. By far the best way to carry on these conversations, as any mountain herdsman or fisherman will tell you, is to sing them. That way the words travel even further and can be understood very well.

There was one famous conversation between a pig keeper from Figari, and his cousin who lived on the northern tip of Sardinia. They hadn't seen each other since a wedding twelve years before but had managed to keep in touch across the straits of Bonifacio. The pig keeper would stand on the cliff at sundown, when the wind was blowing from the North, and sing. When the wind changed direction, he would go back to the cliff at sundown and listen for the response from his cousin. That way both could keep up to date with the to-ings and fro-ings of their extended families.

The cousin was able to warn the pig keeper when pirates were abroad and was the first to know when the vicious winter storms were on their way from the North. When, one evening, the pig keeper began singing of a winged beast with a hunger for fresh fish he was surprised to hear his song repeated all along the coast. In fact, the song became extremely popular and spread right around the coast of Corsica, across the Straits and on around the coast of Sardinia too.

Now as everybody knows, the Sards are extremely competitive, and so their version told of three dragons.

*A city crowded onto clifftops.*

## 78. Of Magical Treasure Chests

Everyone loves a good wedding, whether or not it makes a good marriage and regardless of whether the couple involved have had any say in the matter. While Mandorlinfiore adored Belfioré he never thought himself worthy, even though it might have been his one true wish. Unfortunately, magic sometimes works in unpredictable ways. Don't think that a wish might ever come true in a way that you might expect it to. Magic, by its very nature, is an unreliable element.

You may remember a treasure chest unearthed by mountain pigs and carried to Zonza? The King took a liking to it and had it opened by his locksmith and a new key made. It appeared to be empty, but it was a pretty thing and so the King used it to transport his letter to the Count. While the two brothers travelled together down the mountain to the sea, telling each other stories of what had gone by over the past weeks, the ink on the King's letter woke up, inside the chest, inside the pouch, inside the wallet, behind the waxen seal. The words wandered around on the paper, some letters changing shape, only the signature and the date remained in place.

Neither Mandorlinfiore nor Sylvan noticed anything odd, only Hector the Cat was disturbed by what was going on inside the chest.

'You should open the chest,' said Hector.

'We must respect the King's orders,' said Mandorlinfiore.

'I think he is plotting against you,' said Hector.

'But he loves me,' said Mandorlinfiore.

'He mutters all sorts of things in front of dumb cats,' said Hector, 'I think the word love might be a little optimistic.'

'True,' said Mandorlinfiore, 'he did put me in that big tank when he thought he had lost all that gold. Still, he has lots more now.'

Hector sighed. He turned and tried to ignore the chest. He wondered where his mouse had gone. Pesky mice. He batted at a butterfly, missed, stretched in the afternoon sun and then fell asleep.

## 79. Mustachio'd Bandit Reunion

A dead bandit has an awful lot of time on his hands waiting for the living to sort out their business. If you are not busy robbing travellers, hiding loot, avenging the acts of rival bandits or simply catching wild pigs for supper, then what is a brigand to do? Escobar spent his time collecting songs, listening to singers and memorizing the melodies.

Not all of the singers were flesh and blood either. Roman legionnaires lamented their much-missed homelands of Sparta, Persia and Gaul. Dryads whispered and whistled their own songs, and Escobar paid them all even closer attention, gradually beginning to forget about the world of flesh and blood.

But then the song of the dragon rode along the coast road and Escobar seemed to wake up to the world of the living once again. He wondered whether Fabio and Sandrino had kept up with Mandorlinfiore, and had their business laid to rest, or whether they had become distracted like himself. He had last seen them in the dragon's cavern going silly over the gold.

'If the dragon is now released from her dungeon, then there must be magic abroad in the world,' said Escobar to no one in particular, 'and where there's magic…'

'Escobar?' said Fabio.

'Is that you?' said Sandrino.

'What are you doing here?' said Fabio.

'Waiting for you two,' said Escobar, 'now about that Mandorlinfiore?'

'He's on his way to Bonifacio with a cart load of gold,' said Sandrino.

'Two cart loads,' said Fabio.



## 80. Quarantine?


Belfioré didn't feel like a hostage. She didn't remotely think of herself as a prisoner.

'I am so sorry Princess,' said the Count, 'but there is plague about in the town so you must remain quarantined in the Citadel.'

'Really?' said Belfioré, 'Has anyone told the people of Bonifacio? From what I can see from your battlements they all appear to be going about their normal business.'

'Indeed,' said the Count, 'however, as my guest I must insist that precautions are taken and that you wait another day or two before you set forth.'

'Very well Count,' said Belfioré, 'I will satisfy myself watching the fishermen.'

Belfioré had in fact been watching the fishermen and fisherwomen since she had arrived in Bonifacio and had been listening closely to their songs. From them she too discovered that Rosa-Fury was making something of a nuisance of herself. She wished she could talk to the dragon and help work out a deal which might annoy fewer people.

At the top of the citadel was a high stone watch tower from which you could see the bend in the horizon across the sea. To the South the Sardinian coast was visible, to the north L'Uomo di Cagna and the mountains beyond. From this vantage Belfioré was sure she would be able to catch a glimpse of Rosa-Fury if she was flying nearby. She opened up her poetry book, remembering the time she had spent underground in conversation with the great beast.

## 81. Visitors

The arrival of Mandorlinfiore was supposed to have been low key, just two merchant's carts coming to town on business. However, the King had insisted on sending a small troop of eight men of the Royal Guard just in case the two brothers changed their minds. Belfioré's maid, Maria, had also journeyed with them in a closed carriage in order to escort the Princess safely home.

News of their journey, and impending arrival, had already been doing the rounds of the harbour but only reached the quarantined Citadel when the procession arrived on the quayside.

'I never forgot the sea when I was in the mountains,' said Mandorlinfiore to his brother, 'I don't feel good if I cannot smell the salt air.'

'Our parents and I missed you when you were away,' said Sylvan, 'you didn't seem quite right up in the mountain air. You belong at sea level.'

'Brother, I believe you are right,' said Mandorlinfiore, 'I do not think I will be returning to the King's service. I think I might go to sea.'

'Sir! Sir!' said Escobar as he jumped up in front of the procession waving his head in the air.

'What is the matter Escobar?' said Mandorlinfiore.

'We are returned to your service sir and there are things we must tell you!' said Escobar.

'Very well,' said Mandorlinfiore, 'tell me on the way up to the Count's Citadel.

And so, eight guards, three ghosts, two brothers, a maid and a talking cat, and perhaps his mouse, if he could be found, arrived at the gates of the Citadel of the Count of Bonifacio.

*The high walled citadel.*

## 82. A King's Anticipation

Of the eight men of the King's Guard making up Mandorlinfiore's retinue two were the fastest riders of their company and could get from the port to the Castle of Zonza within a day. The King had instructed them that confirmation of the release of his daughter, while important, was less urgent than news of what happened to his accountant.

Each day that passed heightened the King's anxiety for news, even though he realised that it would take three days for the heavily laden carts to reach Bonifacio. He paced his gold stacked hallways and peered into his gold crammed rooms. As the strong room could never be emptied, he was now reduced to a very few square feet of actual living space. He had no access to his wardrobe and had begun to smell a little off.

The staff hid in the kitchens hoping for something to happen, something that would bring the King to his senses and get the castle back to normal again. But nothing had happened for some time. The gold gathered dust, quite a lot of dust, as the ancient floorboards creaked with the weight of it all.

There was now nothing for the chambermaids to do, as no one could get in to any of the bedrooms, and there was nowhere for the footmen to stand, so as the weather was warm, they all went outdoors and tended to the flower beds and tidied the hedges.

If they looked up at the castle windows, all that could be seen was the colour of the gold as it reflected the sun.

## 83. Arrival at the Citadel

Mandorlinfiore banged on the solid doors of the Citadel. 'I am come by command of the King of Zonza,' said Mandorlinfiore, 'open up at once!'

Immediately the huge doors swung silently open and the procession of King's Men, the carts and the carriage of Maria the maid rolled through.

At once the Count was there to greet them.

'My dear fellows,' said the Count, 'I trust your journey was uneventful?' He clapped his hands and his own guards appeared and took the reins of the cart horses.

'Please be welcome to the Citadel of Bonifacio,' said the Count, 'it is my honour to welcome you here.'

'Sir,' said Mandorlinfiore, 'I believe this chest is for you and that you are already in possession of the key as it was sent by messenger?'

It was true. The Count had the key on a gold chain around his neck, and a good idea of what the King of Zonza's conditions with regard to payment of the ransom were likely to be. All he needed was to unseal the letter and confirm what was required. He took the chest from Mandorlinfiore and handed it to a guard.

'Now what have we got in these carts?' said the Count. He rubbed his hands together and then clapped with delight as each new box of gold was pried open for him to see. When the last one had been inspected, he peeped inside the carriage, 'Well hello there,' said the Count, 'more treasure.'

Maria took the Count's hand and allowed him to help her down the step from the carriage. She was flushed in the face, and his eyes were suddenly very twinkly.

'Let's open this message from the King,' said the Count, 'and then we'll all have some dinner.'

Inside Maria's hat Hector's mouse squeaked with relief. He was starving.

## 84. The Count's Happy Surprise!

The Count showed his guests to their quarters so they could rest and wash before eating. Before he did anything else, he decided it would be prudent to open up the chest and ensure he understood the King's conditions to the letter.

He summoned his Chief Secretary and Master at Arms so that he could enact the orders contained therein. He took the key looped on a golden chain and turned it in the lock. There was a sound like a thousand moths beating their wings and the chest opened.

The Count reached in and retrieved the leather pouch and unstrung it. He took out the silken purse and opened it. He looked closely at the King of Zonza's seal, showed it to his Chief Secretary and his Master at Arms so that they could witness that it was unbroken.

The Count removed the seal and opened up the document. He read through the words on the paper. Then he read them through again. Then he read them through a third time. He handed the letter to his Chief Secretary who also read through it three times. The Master at Arms shrugged.

'Do you want me to chop his head off before dinner?' said the Master at Arms.

'Not today,' said the Count, 'and not tomorrow either!'

The Count clapped his hands and a man servant appeared.

'Tonight, we must roast a dozen geese! Two dozen partridge and three dozen quail!' said the Count, 'Tell the kitchen to prepare a feast!'

'Musicians!' said the Count, 'Send for the musicians, and the juggler, and Gufi my Fool!'

At that moment there came a knocking on the main gate. The gatekeeper peeped out through the spying hatch and saw a Moor with a white ox.

'Good day sir,' said the Moor, 'I do hope I am not late for the wedding?'

## 85. The King of Spain's Daughter

The Kings of Spain, and there have been many great and wise holders of the title, have had many daughters between them. Some have become great and wise Queens in their time, others have become surrounded by intrigue and mystery, and some linked to peculiar trees which bear both pears and nutmegs. Our King of Spain's daughter, Belfioré's mother, was simply lonely and bored at the Court of Zonza.

She was returning from her friends in Florence with a heavy heart. No amount of soft soap, perfumes and lace could keep her entertained for long, and soon it would be winter in the mountains again, with the castle surrounded by wolves and ghosts and bitter winds that battered her windows.

Her ship eased into the Port of Bonifacio past the Circus boats. She loved this island with its dramatic cliffs and sparkling seas.

'If only I didn't have to live in that big dark castle in the mountains,' said the Queen.

'Your Majesty,' said the Ship's Captain, 'I believe the Count of Bonifacio is on the Quayside to greet you.'

This was not unusual. It was, simply, the very best of manners. What was unusual was that the Royal Carriage was not facing the direction of Zonza. As the ship grew closer it became apparent that the Count had such a wide smile on his face it seemed to be split in two.

'What do you suppose is wrong with the Count?' said the Queen, 'I fear I have never seen his face in that contortion in my life.'

It was true. The Count usually wore an expression of mute desperation, but today he looked like he had won a lottery jackpot. Which, in a way, he had. But now he was able to hail the Queen from the quayside.

'Your Majesty!' said the Count. 'You are arrived just in time for our celebrations. Your daughter awaits you atop the citadel.'

And he bowed so low the Queen was afraid he might fall into the harbour.


## 86. Rosa-Fury on the Water


*'When we were a-fishing in the Straits on Tuesday at sunset~*
*A mighty wind bore down upon us from the west~*
*We were more frightened than when the rains rip our sails~*
*It was vast and red and winged with shining scales~*
*We never saw more teeth in a sharks' fierce smile~*
*Believing ourselves soon dead we sung out a-while~*
*And singing we held each other closely in our harmonies~*

*And the beast settled on the waves and said 'more please'~*
*So, we sung our best prize-winning song from last year~*
*Now in this old leather bucket I hold a Dragon's tear~'*

The poetry and music of the fishermen and fisherwomen of Bonifacio tamed the great dragon Rosa-Fury. She chased fish into their nets while they sung laments and drinking songs, love songs and historical ballads recounting great adventures. They were careful to leave out any references to Saint George.


## 87. A Wedding Command


No one was more surprised than Mandorlinfiore by the contents of the King's letter. Well, actually you could have knocked Belfioré down with a feather, and as for the Queen, well she was speechless. The letter read as follows:

*'By order of his most High Majesty, the King of Zonza,*
*the Count of Bonifacio is immediately commanded to join together*
*Princess Belfioré and Mandorlinfiore,*
*who is to become my beloved Regent,*
*in Marriage.'*

Everybody was delighted and the Count very quickly carried out the order, by the power vested in him as Lord Overseer of the Citadel of Bonifacio, counting it very providential that the Queen had appeared just in time to witness the signing of all the deeds.

Everybody gathered at the square overlooking the bay as the sun was riding down the sky toward the horizon. The Count had put on the ancient robes inherited from his great grandfather on his Mother's side, the Grand Vizier of Cairo. However, to let everyone know he was a thoroughbred man of the people he used the traditional language of the people as was the custom at public events. 'By the power vested in my position as Protector of the People of this great City of Bunifaziu, and by Royal Decree request your assent to be married. Do you, Mandorlinfiore of Sulinzano, assent to marry the Princess Belfioré of Zunza?' said the Count.

Mandorlinfiore nodded, 'I must do my duty to the King, and to my heart,' said Mandorlinfiore.

'Do you Princess Belfioré of Zunza, assent to marry Mandorlinfiore of Sulinzano?' said the Count.

Belfioré nodded, 'I must do my duty to the King, and to my heart,' said Belfioré.

'Then I have immense pleasure in pronouncing to the world that these two people are now joined as one in marriage until the end of their days!' said the Count.

A huge cheer rose above the Citadel, and everyone applauded, because we all love a good wedding don't we? Well, most of us do.

The Queen was beside herself with joy. 'You know she turned down Knights and Princes from all over Europe?' said the Queen to the Count.

'I do remember,' said the Count, whose own son had tried and failed. He was happy his wife the Contessa had not lived to see that particular failure. However, Marco was now happily married to a nice young Princess from Napoli.

'I do hope you will stay awhile at my humble Palazzo in the Citadel your Highness?' said the Count.

The Queen, who was never in a hurry to get home said, 'I'd be delighted Count. It is about time I got to know your household again. How is that handsome son of yours?'
'Thank you, your Majesty,' said the Count, 'Marco is very well, thank you, but I am afraid that thanks to him and Princess Marina I am now a silly old grandpapa!'
The two fast riders sent to the city by the King were very pleased to see the King's orders carried out so swiftly and, to their surprise soon found themselves a little too tipsy to attempt the journey to Zonza that evening.

*A mountain city of tall towers.*

## 88. Newlyweds

'What do you think made your Father send this message?' said Mandorlinfiore, 'He made no hint of it, and instead told me we were to discuss a mysterious business venture with the Count.'

'Father has been behaving strangely,' said Belfioré, 'I think he has been driven mad by his gold. The Count has been nothing if not the kindest host, so I can't imagine what mystery there might have been.'

'I did think it strange that he should send his message in the way that he did,' said Mandorlinfiore, 'as I thought he was aware that the chest was not an ordinary thing.'

'My darling,' said Belfioré, 'I believe you have discovered the true reason for the decree.'

Mandorlinfiore remembered then that the chest was supposed to hold the secret to your heart's desire.

'Whatever your Father actually intended, the magic inside the box made sure that~' said Mandorlinfiore.

'~that our heart's desire was actually what happened!' said Belfioré, 'I am very happy dear Mandorlinfiore.'

'I am very happy dear Belfioré.' said Mandorlinfiore. 'But I am not so sure that your Father, the King, will be terribly pleased.'

'Then we must be careful and make sure the messengers cannot leave before we set sail on our honeymoon!' said Belfioré.

'Before we sail anywhere, I fear we have to settle a fair amount of business,' said Mandorlinfiore.

'Of course,' said Belfioré, 'but for now we must dance.'

They danced for as long as the musicians could play, and the musicians played for as long as the newlyweds could dance.

## 89. Of Feasting and Foolery

The feast that followed also became preserved in song. The fowl that the Count had first ordered were never going to satisfy the royal tastes and so he ordered his kitchens to work constantly, producing an endless stream of meats and sweets, salads and puddings.

It was entirely possible, and it is said that this feat was performed successfully by more than one guest, for a person to remain at that banqueting table for three full days and never empty their plate or their glass.

The fireworks set off by the Count's men brought the dragon, Rosa-Fury and her daughter Baba Di Camelo, to the cliff tops to watch. In their excitement they couldn't help but join in with bursts of flame.

The doors to the Citadel were flung open and a three-day Fiesta was declared. There was so much dancing and singing and general merry making that it took another three days for life to return to normal in the city.

The Circus entertainers were retained to perform in the Citadel, and they lit up the ramparts with their displays of fire eating, juggling and breathtaking acrobatics. A high wire was strung across from one battlement to a lookout tower and an acrobat gingerly made his way from one side to the other. All at once a clown ran halfway across while being chased by his friend. He almost fell but caught the rope at the last minute and then pulled himself back up again to cheers from the crowd.

When the clown pulled off his mask he was recognised at once as the Count's very own fool, Gufi. This raised another, even bigger cheer from the crowd who watched as he tiptoed the rest of the way across the high wire.

## 90. Of Guests and Gifts

Mandorlinfiore and Belfioré were amazed and happy to be married and began their life together as husband and wife at the top of the tallest tower in the Citadel. Here they received visits and gifts from all of the local dignitaries. Even Mandorlinfiore's adoptive parents made the journey from Solenzara. Everyone was welcomed.

After a little while it became clear that the King of Zonza would soon hear of the fantastic festivities that had taken place and would have to respond. He would not hear from his wife, the Queen, as she had no intention of making the climb into the dark interior when everything was so bathed in light in Bonifacio.

One fine afternoon a local fisherman made the climb up from the harbour with four of his thirteen children, Abel, Beulah, Carlo and Diana. They brought with them their songs, with which they had seduced a dragon, who, they said, was less fierce than the judges at the singing festival. Mandorlinfiore loved singing and had always enjoyed listening to the songs sung on the quayside while he inspected bright new cloth from Genoa, or fresh spices from Carthage. He would hum along and then sing the songs back to himself when he was in the bath.

After the old fisherman and his children had sung a good few songs Mandorlinfiore asked if he could join them.

'I have a passable voice,' said Mandorlinfiore, 'but have only had the pleasure of singing alone, and it would be a joy to sing with a group as fine as yours.'

'We would be honoured your Highness,' said the old fisherman.

And so Mandorlinfiore stood with the five singers and sung a mournful lament of love lost at sea, which made Belfioré want to weep. As her hot salt tears filled her eyes, she seemed to see Mandorlinfiore's features reform and merge with those of the four younger singers until she could not tell which one was her husband. She blinked and wiped her eyes and there he was again.

When the song was ended Mandorlinfiore was so happy he was in tears.

'That was the best gift of all,' said Mandorlinfiore, and he shook the old fisherman by the hand. He gave the fisherman a close look, 'I do believe I know you from somewhere.' said Mandorlinfiore.

'Yes. I believe we met once, a very long time ago,' said the old fisherman, 'but I expect you will have seen us at a Fiesta, singing at a competition.'

'Of course,' said Mandorlinfiore, 'where we shall see and hear you all again.'

Belfioré couldn't speak and just smiled and waved as the singers left the chamber.


## 91. Who Will Tell the King?


The two King's Men, the fastest riders on the mountains (but never quite as fast as Belfioré and her white mare) were pushing their horses to the limit as they climbed into the dark heart of Zonza. The forest closed in on either side, the air grew colder, and the horses couldn't help but slow.

'We should not have feasted so much,' said Paolo, 'I will have to fast for days to fit my breeches properly again.'

'You are right,' said Ricardo, 'I am so tired from all the dancing that my legs feel like they are made of rocks.'

'It has been a week already,' said Paolo, 'the King is going to be furious enough at our delay.'

'You are right,' said Ricardo, 'he will punish us for not leaving immediately.'

'What if some minstrel or vagabond has spread the news of the wedding?' said Paolo, 'The King might know already and then what?'

'We will be in the dungeons,' said Ricardo, 'or worse.'

'We have to do something,' said Paolo.

'Do what?' said Ricardo, 'I believe we are doomed.'

'But what if we were attacked?' said Paolo, 'You know what this stretch of road is like for bandits?'

'You are right,' said Ricardo, 'We could have been lying by the roadside for days, our battered and broken bodies eyed by vultures.'

'Maybe not quite as bad as that,' said Paolo, 'but they might have taken our horses all the same.'

'Good idea,' said Ricardo, 'and we are less than half a day's walk to the castle. Let's turn the horses loose.'

'I agree,' said Paolo, 'they will find their way home on their own, but we must tie them to a tree so they cannot follow.'

'But wait,' said Ricardo, 'I don't think I can walk anywhere. What if we escaped our attackers? Maybe we saw them off and are late because we had a duty to make the road to Zonza safer?'

'Then we would be heroes,' said Paolo, 'instead of fools.'

'You are right,' said Ricardo, 'now hit me.'

'Why would I do that?' said Paolo.

'To make our battle with bandits more convincing,' said Ricardo.

The two men dismounted and tied their horses then stood facing each other. Paolo began by slapping Ricardo on the left cheek. Ricardo responded with a back-hand slap across Paolo's right cheek.

'That's not going to convince anyone,' said Paolo, and he landed a blow on Ricardo's right eye.

'You are right,' said Ricardo, and he threw a punch that nearly dislodged Paolo's teeth.

'That's better,' said Paolo as he targeted Ricardo's other eye.

'You are right,' said Ricardo as he ducked, 'but I've had enough of us punching each other. I think we can do better punching ourselves. It will save our friendship.'

'You are right Ricardo,' said Paolo, 'and we must tear our clothes and roll on the ground in the dirt as well to make it look like a proper struggle.'


## 92. Mustachio'd Bandits Abroad


Meanwhile, not so very far off in the forest, a small band of mustachio'd bandits watched in wonder as two of the King of Zonza's personal guard had the oddest fight they had ever seen.

'It must be a trap,' said Baldino, the leader of this particular band of mustachio'd bandits.

'Perhaps they are drunk?' said Angelo, his second in command.

'Nico and Tuco, you must go to steal their horses. Angelo and me, we will have some fun with these fools,' said Baldino.

Nico and Tuco crept silently through the forest and slipped the reins of the horses. At the same time Baldino and Angelo called and hollered in the other direction.

'My leg! My leg! It's broken!' said Baldino, in a voice so full of anguish that even the dryads heard him.

It did the trick as both Paolo and Ricardo left off their rolling in the dirt and came to investigate. At once they were caught and tied at wrist and ankle and bound to an ancient olive tree.

'Look!' said Baldino, 'We have caught ourselves two of the King's Men. Two rather fat and slow King's Men it must be said but still we must have our trophies.'

'What will you do to us?' asked Ricardo.

'We will take your clothes,' said Baldino, 'they will make a good disguise. We already have your horses.'

'Can we have their boots too?' said Angelo.

'Yes,' said Baldino, 'why not?'

'And their swords?' said Angelo.

'It would be rude not to steal everything they have,' said Baldino, 'I couldn't bear it.'

And so, they stripped the King's Men of their fine uniforms and well-made boots leaving them tied to the olive tree in just their undergarments.

'Well I think we slipped up there,' said Paolo, 'but I guess we won't have to make up any stories now.'

'You are right,' said Ricardo.

'It's starting to get dark,' said Paolo, 'and I believe there may be wolves over this side of the forest.'


## 93. A Dangerous Hoard


Gold, as you may know from science class, or perhaps you are a Prince or Princess and have gold bars lying around all over the place, is heavy. It is difficult to transport large amounts as it takes a lot of effort to lift a large chest full of gold, and if your belt is not of the best quality, when you fill your pockets with gold coins, your trousers may well fall down.

If you were to stack your upstairs bedroom, in your nice normal house, from floor to ceiling with chests brimming with gold, so that you could only get to your bed if you wriggled sideways through a narrow gap, and you had to forget about your chest of drawers altogether, then the floor would need quite a lot of extra support.

Even if you live in a massive tall castle built of iron black stone with floors made of chestnut boards, there is a limit to the amount of weight you can expect it to comfortably take. The King was not an engineer. He had not built the castle, and no one in Zonza could remember a time without it. But now, every floor of the castle was stacked to the ceiling with gold, every room was crammed, even the servant's quarters and the kitchens.

All of the King's staff had moved out into the village, and some had left for more sane employment elsewhere. The King was the only person left in the castle, and he would worm his way around the treasure chests, crawl over gold bars up the stairs and squeeze out onto the highest battlements at the top of the castle, where he would watch for the return of his men.

One late afternoon he spotted Paolo and Ricardo. They were riding in with one of his patrols and looked to have been molested by brigands. Never mind that, he thought, and signalled to them from the top of the tower.

Paolo caught his eye, looked back at Ricardo, who shrugged, and then began signing the news of the wedding.

'What?' signed the King, 'Are you joking? I will cut off your heads!' The King drew his hand across his throat to make sure they understood.

Paolo and Ricardo both signed the same message, and then shrugged.

The King was mad with rage. He stamped and stamped and tore his hair. His face grew first red, then magenta, and then purple. People who saw this display were convinced that steam was bursting from his ears. In actual fact, it was dust.

The ancient castle could take no more. The timbers on the top floor gave way and collapsed onto the floor below with an almighty bang. Moments later the floor below also gave way, crashing through the next floor. The iron black stone walls began to crumble as the castle fell in upon itself.

The roof disappeared into the tower, the walls falling in on top.

It was spectacular. Within minutes the Castle of Zonza had completely disappeared into a hole in the ground, taking the King and his vast hoard of gold with it. No one ever saw the King again, and stories of the great cavern below the town of Zonza eased into legend and are now almost entirely forgotten.

However, should you ever be lucky enough to visit the beautiful village of Zonza, and should stumble upon the entrance to a cave, and suspect that there might be a great hoard of gold at the end of it, just remember that an enormous dragon and her child might well be sleeping right on top of it.


## 94. Long Live the King and Queen


'But how can I be King without a castle?' said Mandorlinfiore, 'I have no fortune and no desire to rule or tell people what they should or should not do.'

'But what about protection of the people from pirates and bandits?' said the Count, 'This is what taxes are for? You can stay here at the Citadel.'

'Can we garrison the King's Men here too?' said Mandorlinfiore, 'I believe Zonza is reduced to a village.'

'Of course! Zonza was never really best placed as a centre of Government, and you are a sensible man, good with numbers. There is a lot of trade here, between us we could turn Bonifacio into a very dynamic place!' said the Count, getting rather excited.

'Without a castle to support taxes could be lowered,' said Mandorlinfiore, 'with just the one main port we could be the gateway to the Tyrhennian Sea!'

'Now you are talking like a King!' said the Count.

'But what about the Queen of Zonza?' said Mandorlinfiore.

'I am thinking about asking her to become my new Contessa,' said the Count, 'Following a suitable period of mourning for the old King of course.'

'A week?' said Mandorlinfiore.

'Yes,' said the Count, 'that should do it. Actually, I must be completely honest, I have already asked her, and she has already said yes. I could not be happier!'

'My Husband!' said Belfioré, who had been out on the battlements with her Mother, 'I want to go sailing with you amongst the islands.'

'We will,' said Mandorlinfiore, 'as soon as I have taken care of one or two matters of business I cannot put off.'

'I do not want to be like the rulers my parents were.' said Belfioré, 'My Father the King was all work, and my Mother the Queen was all play.'

'No, said Mandorlinfiore, 'we will be together as much as possible from now on. We cannot be separated by seas or mountains. When you are sailing a ship on the crest of a wave, I will be with you, when you are riding a horse on the peak of a mountain, we will be together.'

# 95. Unfinished Bandit Business

'Now he is King he will be too busy to think about us,' said Fabio.

'I don't know about that,' said Escobar, 'everyone seems to want to do everything for you if you are the King.'

'Then perhaps he can tell someone else to help us?' said Sandrino.

'I'm sure he will,' said Escobar.

So Escobar, Sandrino and Fabio went to see Mandorlinfiore, who wrote down their requests, as no one else could see or hear them, and ordered his men to ride out to the Bay of Rondinaria, the rock outcrop of L'Uomo di Cagna, and the Stone Fields of Filitosa. They returned, after some time, with three boxes of treasure. Escobar's was the most impressive, but he had been in this particular job for longer than the others.

Mandorlinfiore had the three treasure chests put in a private room and arranged to meet the three ghostly mustachio'd bandits. He showed the bandits their loot.

'Here is your legacy in this life,' said Mandorlinfiore, 'what will you have me do with it?'

'Take it and give it to help the poor,' said Escobar, 'It might make up for the bad things I have done, after all I poisoned my two young friends.'

'That is very noble of you Escobar,' said Mandorlinfiore, 'I will make sure that your wishes are respected, your family cared for and I thank you for all your help up to now.'

'Thank you,' said Escobar, and he suddenly shimmered and sparkled and then was gone.

Sandrino and Fabio watched with fascination. While they had enjoyed 'ghosting' as they had called it, creeping up on people and ruffling their hair with a haunted breeze, that was about as far as their fun went. Apart from

Mandorlinfiore, no one else was aware they even existed, which was very frustrating.

'Take my booty and use it to make amends,' said Sandrino. 'Mine too,' said Fabio, 'after all, we did chop off poor old Escobar's bonce.'

'Thank you both,' said Mandorlinfiore, 'I will make sure all three of you are commemorated for the good works you did after your deaths, and that your families are cared for.'

'Thank you,' said both Fabio and Sandrino together, then they shimmered and sparkled and were gone.

*A Corsican beach.*

## 96. Of Dragons and Sorcerers

And so, it would seem that Rosa-Fury had given her daughter a name that was wholly inappropriate for a winged scaly fire breathing beast. But she did not care, for Baba de Camelo was gorgeous, and had a squishy tummy and everything a mother dragon could desire.

Baba' was good in the air too and rarely bumped into mountain tops when they flew out together. They had enjoyed the fireworks at the wedding and had smiled and wept at the songs sung by the fishermen and fisherwomen. However, when her hoard of gold crashed back into her cavern, Rosa-Fury realised that the time had come again to retreat from the world of people.

People always brought danger with them, and now that her Baba' was out of the egg, Rosa-Fury wanted to make sure that she grew up the way a dragon should, out of sight. They began to fly only at night, and would fish far out to sea, away from the boats of Bonifacio and as far from the trade routes as they could get.

Before long they would pass once more into folklore as the people on the island got on with their own daily tasks, remembering them only when the songs were sung at the festivals. There was just the one visit left to make, to the top tower of the Citadel at Bonifacio.

When the Castle of Zonza collapsed and began its journey into legend, it woke up an old magic that had been sitting very still for thirty years upon the ramparts. What many had taken to be a rather odd carved stone, was in fact the Mazerre, who had aided the King's cause at the beginning. There was nothing that the Mazerre liked less than dragons. He had taken great pleasure in the locking up of Rosa-Fury all those years ago, and the gradual, stealthy removal of a tiny proportion of her hoard. But it had taken an awful lot of hard work to achieve, which is why he had slept so long.

The Mazerre was a sorcerer of the old magic and had wrestled dragons and sea serpents, winged harpies and stone giants. There was little left in the world that could scare him. He knew what his strengths had been in the old days, but now he worried about the weakness of his advanced years. It had been a long time since the last battle and so it was that he sought to call in his favours and ask for reinforcements, just in case.

He called for the King of the Animals. But he did not come. He was cleaning his pizza ovens.

He called for the Black Hart. But the White Hart barred the way.

He called for the Dryads, who had been burned to the ground by so many dragons before, but they were still grumbling over the King of the Animals.

He called his own tribe of Mazerre, but they were all so tired from the last great battle that their stone ears couldn't hear him.

So that was it. This old Mazerre would have to take care of the dragon on his own. He sat in the cold sun on the top of mount Zonza and sharpened his claws.

## 97. Let Battle Commence

A dragon is an elite predator, at the top of the chain. If there was something else out there that would want to kill and eat a dragon it could only be another, bigger, hungrier dragon. It is the same with the lion today. What on earth would want to eat a lion?

150

A human on a horse, with a lance and armour might have a slim chance if the dragon was as small as Baba de Camelo or was old or tired or ill or injured by some misjudged landing or fight with another dragon. A full-grown beast, with no such handicap, would only ever be vulnerable to the most cunning Mazerre.

While Rosa-Fury was out fishing and Baba de Camelo was playing with the hoard of gold in the cavern, the Mazerre seized his chance and ran down the mountain toward the mouth of the cavern. He raised a thin column of dust as he ran and dislodged massive boulders on his way which he piled up in front of the entrance to the dragon's lair.

Rosa-Fury spotted the dust cloud and knew instinctively that something bad was happening. She swooped down and filled the valley floor with flame. The Forest of Zonza cried out and the Dryads fled for shelter. The Mazerre turned himself to stone and hid among the boulders. He glowed red but did not burn. He remained still and waited. Rosa-Fury blasted the boulders away from the entrance but spotted the Mazerre in his disguise. Furious, she picked him up, wrapping her talons around him.

'I was Rosa-Fury, and Goldentail, and before that I was Rock-Scorcher, and before that I was Fiery-Death, but now I am Nightmare and taking me on is the last thing you will remember,' said the dragon and she flew up through the clouds as high as she could go, and then on into the sky.

The Mazerre worked to make himself as heavy as he could, but as he shrunk into an ever-denser ball so Nightmare's talons closed tighter around him.

The dragon struggled higher and higher until she could see the entire outline of the island of Corsica. On she went, until the stars began to appear, even though it was the middle of the morning.

The Mazerre shrunk himself down to the size of a marble and Nightmare had to let him go. As soon as he was free, he was able to return to his original form. He caught hold of her right heel talon to stay out of range and extended his own razor-sharp claws and lunged at the dragon's belly. One pierced her scales and she let out a shriek of pain. She beat her wings and tried to pull free of the earth's gravity. The Mazerre could feel dragons' blood slowly trickle along his arm. He twisted his claw deeper, anchoring himself firmly to his prey. He was happy now. This dragon could fly him to the moon for all he cared. She was his now.


## 98. A Brief History of Dragons and Mazerre


A lot has been said over the time it has taken to tell this story about the mysteries of Magic. Old Magic, the Ancient Ways, Magic of plants and animals, Magic of Moors and their Beasts.

The King of the Animals has been around, weaving his illusions, devising and setting curses, enslaving Princes and beggars for as long as anyone can remember. He is to be discovered in some of the very oldest stories.

These are the stories of the world from when it was almost new, when the world was ruled by dragons and people were only a small hidden part of things.

In those days people were protected by the King of the Animals, while the dragons fought amongst themselves. Some say that it was their own blood lust which finished off the dragons and forced them underground. Others tell stories of a rock that fell to earth from the heavens and covered the world in a dust cloud which blocked out the sun for so long the dragons died of the cold.

A few stories claim that there was a great battle between dragons and Mazerre which ended up in both species decimated to the point of near extinction. There are fewer stories surrounding the origins of the Mazerre. While we can all go to a museum in our capital cities and see the bones of dead dragons on display in great halls, nowhere are there displays of the ancient remains of the shape shifting Mazerre.

One story tells of how there was once a twin planet to ours, blue and green like ours, full of abundant life and wondrous magical beasts, like ours. This is where the Mazerre were born, and where they had to escape from after a terrible event which turned their home into a rocky red desert.

If you were to come across a Mazzerri, or Mazzerru today they would look a lot like you and I. This is because the original Mazerre now live in the shadow lands of our dreams and Corsican men and women find themselves called in their sleep.

They travel to a parallel world to do battle with each other for the souls of their fellow villagers. They will hunt wild boar in their dreams and if successful the boar will at once reveal itself to be a villager, who will most certainly be dead before a year goes by.

Few people enjoy the call of the Mazerre, while some have managed to escape. One day they will only ever exist in stories, until then, if you should be fortunate enough to find yourself in Corsica, and are settling down for the night just now, in your sleeping bag, or in your villa or hotel room, do remember to say your prayers.

# 99. Sailing Away

'Are you certain this is what you want to do brother?' said Sylvan.

'I am a King and my Queen wishes to see the world,' said Mandorlinfiore, 'so we must go. You have the ear of the Count. He is a good man and used to running things. All will be well.'

'My dear husband,' said Belfioré, 'we must go. We will see Sylvan, and everyone else again soon.'

They set off, alone in their single-masted ship, with no spectral mustachio'd bandits, no Palace Guards, no maids or manservants, bound for wherever the wind would take them, held up by the sea, just under the sky.

'I want to see what is at the other end of the sea,' said Belfioré, 'I want to see the sights the ancient poets have written their songs for. I want us to see deserts and dolphins, gods and giants, sunsets and stars yet to be mapped.'

'Then that is what we will do,' said Mandorlinfiore.

Down below decks Hector the cat was curled up on the featherbed in the cabin. 'As long as they don't get me wet, then they can go anywhere they like,' said Hector, 'at least the fish will be fresh.'

He batted his mouse.

'Stop it,' said the mouse.

Hector gave his mouse a look and licked his lips.

'No, no. Bat away,' said the mouse, 'don't mind me.'

Hector blinked and purred.

Up on deck Mandorlinfiore and Belfioré unfurled the sails and the little ship caught hold of the wind and began to run out of the harbour, past the cliffs of Bonifacio and the Capo Bianco on toward the Isle di Lavezzi, then beyond into the Tyrhennian Sea. The Queen and the Count watched from the Citadel, and the Moor caught a glimpse from the top of the Capo.

After a little while sailing, Mandorlinfiore and Belfioré met with a Pharaoh and visited her Temples and Pyramids. They crossed the desert on camels and took tea with the King of Ethiopia. Their little ship took them across another sea to a land where the people were ruled by a God who had the head of an elephant on his shoulders. Further on they were able to map the stars of a new zodiac, they saw a volcano explode on the horizon and walked upon a newly born island. While they were lucky not to meet any sea monsters, there was a narrow escape from a tribe of giants.
Eventually their ship found its way back to port in Bonifacio where not much had changed. In their absence the Count had been able to put up a charming palazzo for the retuned King and Queen on the quayside. They were able to move straight in, but never really settled down.


100. Of Fire and Ice


There comes a point, should you fly high enough, where gravity loosens its grip. It is unheard of for any creature to fly as high as that as the air is so very thin. However, if you are a dragon, and are furious enough, and happen to hit just the right angle at the right speed, and you are good at holding your breath, then you may find yourself in a low orbit.
On the edge of space, it is extremely cold, much colder than a frosty day, colder even than the mountain tops of Zonza in the deepest of winters. If you are a Mazerre,

attached to an orbiting dragon, then you would need every last ounce of magic to survive. It is so cold that it can make the water inside a person's bones begin to freeze, which is exactly what began to happen to the Mazerre.

Nightmare, the Dragon, was not spared the discomfort but was able to burn a little flame between her jaws in order to keep the ice at bay. Beyond this, staying aloft now took little effort, while forward speed began to rise at an extraordinary pace. Below them Europe and Persia sped past, then India and China, the Pacific Ocean and the Americas, and then again and again, each time more rapidly than the last.

The Mazerre was only just aware of what was going on. His thoughts focussed on the tiny bit of warmth left in the claw he had embedded in the dragon's belly.

It might be cold in space but re-entering the Earth's atmosphere is tricky and can involve some extremely high temperatures. Of course, had you also sported names such as Rock-Scorcher or Fiery-Death then this would hold absolutely no fear for you at all. Nightmare enjoyed extreme heat and the change from sub-zero to super-hot came as a very welcome change.

For the Mazerre, on the other hand, a different reaction, a defensive response. He withdrew his claw and became a rock, hard and dense as the granite outcrops of Corsica. Down he fell, faster than the dragon. She slowed, the air was thickening, buoying her up under her wings. Nightmare watched as the Mazerre dropped.

He hit the ground by Filitosa on the South West coast of Corsica and shattered into a thousand pieces.

Today the area is full of menhirs, some with the evil eye carved into them, others marked with the face of a man, gazing up toward the sky. Some say the stones have healing properties, while others report frightening dreams after a visit. Some say that if you visit at dawn on midsummer's day you can hear the cry of the ancient Mazerre as the sun rises.

And the Dragon? She was careful never to be seen again, and she did try very hard to be invisible, but she was not always completely successful as she did enjoy the singing festivals so much.

## 101. A Ship Departs

A great trading ship is preparing to sail from the harbour. Its sails are being made ready and there are ribbons and buntings dressing the rigging. All in all, it is a very festive occasion. On board there are many travellers and traders and one or two dignitaries, and below deck there is a white ox amongst the creatures bedded down for the journey.

But none of this concerns us at the moment. If you may remember from the beginning of our story, in this town it was the custom for the husband to stand at the door, ready to announce to the community the name and status of the new arrival. Our young husband had been on tenterhooks all night long. He longed for a son or daughter he could take to sea or ride out with across the mountains. In this town, as you will recall, it was also the custom that whoever might be passing the front door at the moment of the child's birth would bestow their particular fate upon the baby. To counter this, it was usual for the family's friends to guard the door so that no undesirable persons may come anywhere near.

This very morning all of Mandorlinfiore's brothers and friends were gathered on the quayside in front of his house, while all of Belfioré's family and friends were gathered inside. It was too early for pirates and brigands to be abroad. It was too early for the slavers and the madams, but wait, who was that galloping so urgently across the flagstones on his fine black horse?

And the husband called out to his wife, 'Not yet, not yet.'

But that's another story...

# Sir Guillaume de Saint Hilaire

'Bonjour mes amis, let me tell you, I was once a young person it is true. Certainly, it was a long time ago that I first skipped onto a horse's back and galloped from chateau to village, village to town, town to chateau. No, I do not think much of dashing away on new adventures these days. I have had my time wandering the wilder paths of this world.

You see, from this window I can watch the sun arrive on the sea and, later, hide behind the mountain, ships come and go, grand carriages and old wagons roll past, each one on their way to their own adventure, stories writ large in the lines on the faces of Captains and cowherds.

But I do not imagine many will encounter the sights, the creatures, or the people that I did when I was abroad. In those days I had a fine black Percheron whom I named Baucent in honour of the greatest knight of all. I adorned him with crimson blankets and a saddle of the finest quality from Córdoba.

When I was still a whelp, I grew tired of galloping in circles and longed for a life of adventure. My father, the Duc de Saint Hilaire, was a wise man and had trained my older brother Abelard in the safe administration of his lands. My next brother, Bernard, was a stoic deputy, then Charles, the priest, Denis, the brewer, Etienne, the farmer, Frederic, the other farmer, then me, the wild boy.

My mother, the Duchess, was wiser than my father and had me indentured to her brother Knight when I was eleven years old. Sir Thibaut d'Evreaux was the finest swordsman the King had ever had, so they said, and an accomplished leader of men in his own day.

But this is not his story, nor is it the story of my family, it is not even the whole story, for there would never be time for that. Instead I will tell you of the time I first laid eyes upon the Citadel at Bonifacio on the southern coast of the island of Corsica, and the strange adventure that was to follow.

I had been to pay my respects at Santiago di Compostela and was on a ship, set sail from Barcelona. I was not on my way to Bonifacio, I was on my way to Rome, and then on to the Holy Land, but as it was, the ship had to put-in to harbour for other travellers and for good commercial reasons.

I was astonished at the sight of the town houses crowded along the top of the cliff as if ready to dive into the sea. A man might simply cast a line from his bed in order to catch supper for his family.

Our Captain told us we were to remain in town for a week or two for repairs, and to await a boat from Sardinia. There was wine on its way that was said to be an aid to long life and good health. The Sards would swear by it and claim to remember being at events long ago that the people of Corsica only heard about from their great-Grandparents.

The wise know that absurd rivalries exist wherever a nameplate will define one parish from another, for folk can be foolish over the smallest things, and so it was that I heard a tale in a tavern in the Citadel of Bonifacio that a race of giants lived deep in the mountainous interior of Corsica. Taller than any person to be found anywhere they were, least of all on the island of Sardinia, where all were mere dwarfs and pygmies.

My curiosity grew with every goblet of the good wine poured in that hostelry and, at midnight, I set off, past the tiny fishermen's hovels and into the forested road that led into the mountains. There was a moon to light my way and owls and other night birds to amuse my ears. I had heard rumours of monsters and bandits and other beasts, but I feared nothing in those days.

My horse, having been stabled in the darkened bowels of the traders' ship for eight days was ready for a good long run and he flew through the forest, through the foothills and up into the mountains whinnying with joy. I confess, I had not enjoyed the confinement of the crossing either,

161

and so I drew in the mountain air with happiness in my heart.

When the sun rose into the pale morning sky both Baucent and I began to tire. At that moment we spied an Inn with a well-dressed gentleman awaiting at the door, but I had heard tell of this establishment in the tavern and we galloped past without hesitation and headed into a stand of chestnut trees. Here we rested through the heat of the day, listening to the soft whisper of the wind as it took its stories around the island.

I was well provisioned and felt no need to feast at any tavern or other place and while I lay my head against the root of a tree I watched as customers arrived, but I never once saw one leave. As night fell Baucent and I rode on through the cool dark mountains, coming upon a walled city with a castle rising at its heart as black as iron. We did not stop but ventured further into the dark interior.

Every time we crested a ridge there was a higher one rising before us, but Baucent was not disheartened and instead seemed more eager than I to rise to the top of the next pass. Once more, as the sky brightened toward dawn, a place of rest appeared, a moss-covered hillock next to a tall, slender waterfall. We stopped and I made camp, Baucent drinking deeply of the clear mountain water.

The world is a much more dangerous place than you can imagine, and I say this because it is everywhere. I have seen it at Carnac on the road through the Vannetais to Cornouaille, silent green spaces that harbour faeries and worse, who will steal your senses and all that you care for in this life. I should have known better of course but I laid my head down to sleep without a second thought.

All at once I set to dreaming that I was safe at home and that Blancheflor, my beloved first love from when I was but a small boy, was singing a story of Guillaume d'Orange. I always enjoyed the old stories and never tired of hearing them. However, this became a version I had not heard before and when I noticed this, I saw that Blancheflor had transformed into someone else. The slender yellow-haired girl had become a dark-skinned Saracen woman, tall, elegant and armed as if she were going to an assassination.

I reached for the pommel of my sword, but it was not in its scabbard. I looked for it and saw that it was standing upright on top of the mossy hillock. The woman opened her mouth to speak and a foul smoke poured forth from between her lips that caused me to cough and choke the smell was so awful. I clasped a hand across my own mouth so as not to draw in any of that pestilential stink and reached for my sword with the other.

At once I was frozen to the spot, cursing my luck and praying to all the saints for deliverance from this devil-magic. I felt my toes grow long and burst through the ends of my boots and curl around the rocks and stones beneath my feet. Leaves sprouted at the end of my nose making it hard for me to see what was happening. I grew taller and began to sway as I was nudged by the song of the wind. All this time the foul smoke spiralled around me spreading the enchantment into which I had become bound.

My eyes parted company and became lookouts both North and South in two opposite directions. I could see that on one side I had green shoots appearing all over my body and on the other that my arms had become gnarled with the pattern of bark. Then I saw a tree standing next to me that wore such a terrible and sad expression that it moved me almost to tears. That this was my destiny I could not countenance.

Then from below I heard the whinny of my horse Baucent, another rider was approaching at a gallop, the hoofbeats echoing in the forest. A war cry sounded, peculiarly high-pitched, an ululation that reminded me of the courageous crusading nuns who I once saw battle the

Turks in the savage North African desert (but that is a story for another time).

It was all of a hurry and a terrible rush, but I swear it was a girl-child that struck down the fearsome incarnation that tortured me so. Behind her flew a hawk, who caught up a veil, unwound the apparition and broke the spell. I blinked and then discovered myself upon my backside next to the stream, my sword laid out beside me. Of the child and the peculiar woman there was no sign.

I wasted not a minute more and, thanking the saints for my miraculous deliverance climbed once again into the saddle that has been a more reliable and comfortable home for so long. Together Baucent and I continued our journey deeper into the mountain stronghold of the island, deeper into the deadly magic of the place, but confident now that we were protected in our quest by forces that desired our success.

At the close of what I counted as the third day of our journey I spied a dwelling built against a massy outcrop of rock. It had a tall door and a high-set window and a chimney, from which a plume of white woodsmoke curled into the clear evening sky. A tree trunk leaned against the wall next to the door and as I drew closer, I saw that it was as long as I was tall. This, I reasoned, had to be the home of a giant. I approached with caution for giants, as you should know, are remarkably bad tempered.

I dismounted and let Baucent graze on the grasses and wildflowers at the side of the track and used the sword pommel to rap on the door. Giants are usually hard of hearing too, so I made sure to knock as loud as I could. Almost at once I heard a response from the high window, 'Who dares disturb Gregor the Great?'

'It is I, Sir Guillaume of Saint Hilaire, servant of God and the King of France,' I said.

'Go away or I will squash you with my club,' came the reply.

'I am here in good faith and only wish to pay my compliments,' I said.

'I will count to three,' came the reply.

'I assure you by the hairs on my chin that I do not wish to harm you sir,' I said.

'I will count to three again,' came the reply.

'I am a travelling knight on his way to the Holy Land through Santiago di Compostela and Rome merely in search of good company on the way sir,' I said.

All at once there came a tugging on my surcoat. I looked down and met the bright blue eyes of a tiny man the size of a child but with a beard that was as red as the flames on a coal fire.

'Bring your horse around the side to the stables, but be quick,' he said.

I did as I was told and followed the curious little fellow past the giant's club and in between a collection of enormous boulders that had been rounded so that they resembled a set of gigantic marbles.

'Throwing stones,' said the tiny man in response to my curious glances, 'stones for throwing'.

He led Baucent and I into a well-cared for stable in which two donkeys and a pony were already berthed. The straw was fragrant and there was food ready for my horse too. I hesitated for a moment but remembered that there is an unmistakeable smell to magic and I was certain I could not detect it here.

Once I had settled Baucent and seen how the stable door was secured I followed my miniature host through a door and found myself all at once inside the home of the giant who called himself Gregor the Great. There was a giant chair with a seat the same height as my head and a bed that was built across the entire width of the house.

'Where is the giant?' I said.

The tiny man looked me up and down and shook his head, then pointed at a long narrow ladder that was propped against the wall. It led to the high window where I could see a small chair and a stack of little notebooks.

'You are the giant?' I said.

'Not as stupid as you look,' he said, 'sorry, but a lot of the knights I have met have not been as polite as you.'

'Gregor the Great,' I said, 'I am very pleased to meet you.'

'Likewise, Sir Guillaume of Saint Hilaire,' said Gregor, 'So tell me the news of the wide world while I finish making stew. You do like stew?'

And so, I spent a mostly agreeable evening with the smallest giant in the world, recounting stories of my travels in many wild and strange countries from the Danish forests to the mountains of Morocco, the frozen plains of Russia and the glittering mythical islands of Greece. For his part Gregor maintained his illusion of bad-tempered giant-hood in order to fend off a tribe of actual giants who lived behind the next two mountains to the North.

The house had belonged to a giant many years before Gregor had arrived to claim the dwelling as his own, but the name of this giant was long forgotten. My tiny host spent his days writing poetry, sitting in his high window, some of which he recited for my entertainment. I have heard many a rousing song and tear making poem in my years here on God's earth, but I can honestly say that I had never heard such terrible poetry.

My winces he took as smiles of approval and so continued to recite even as the last flames of the fire began to gutter and my eyes closed. I might guess that he must have continued while I slept, hearing my snores as cheers and grunts of pleasure at his destruction of his mother-tongue and mutilation of words.

Nevertheless, I awoke refreshed and steady in the morning, looking forward to encountering true giants hiding out in their stronghold in the heart of this mysterious island. I declined an offer of breakfast so keen was I to resume my quest. I found Baucent well rested and it was not long before I could bid farewell to our host.

'Who among these giants is their chieftain?' I asked.

'I cannot tell you,' said Gregor the Great.

'Why not?' I asked.

'Because I have never met any giant apart from you and you seem small for a giant.' He said.

'So how is it that you are so certain that the giants are your neighbours?' I said.

'I am not certain of anything,' he said, 'I am not certain that when you turn the next corner in the road ahead that you will continue to exist.'

'Whyever would you think that?' I said.

'Because I will not be able to see you,' he said, 'and seeing is believing is it not? You saw my tall house with its high window and believed a giant must live here.'

'That is true, but are you telling me that you have never met a giant from the mountains?' I said.

'I have never met anyone at all,' he said, 'not since I arrived here thirty years ago.'

'Are you not curious?' I said.

'A little,' he said.

'Then saddle up your pony and come with me,' I said.

'But will it be dangerous?' he said.

'I should hope so,' I said.

The morning had a refreshing chill to it and I observed that we were on a road that travelled above a sea of fog, reducing the island to the few peaks that I could see ahead, with an archipelago of smaller peaks strung out to the South behind us. The land grew rockier and the trees smaller and scrubbier the higher we climbed. The chill bit deeper and I expected to see snow at any point. Behind me Gregor the Great kept pace on his pony.

Up ahead I saw an enormous eagle take flight. It spread its wings and rode a current of air that took it so far up into the sky that it was turned into the tiniest speck of black against the pale blue heavens. The wind whistled a soft tune that made my eyes water with its cold caress.

Gregor was a good riding companion. He had grown used to not talking over the years, and so I was spared the idle chatter that can sometimes spoil a good day. Neither did he hum or sing, but I doubt whether this was courtesy as he did seem rather easily startled by the most commonplace of things most likely borne of his long confinement.

At last we crested the mountain and riding down the leeward side I spied an abandoned herder's shelter. To the inexperienced eye it simply looked like a stack of rocks rolled there by weather and earthquakes, but to me it looked like a mansion. There was room enough for our mounts to shelter alongside us and so we made our supper and we set to sleep.

When I awoke, I knew it was the morning, but the light was different and strangely bright. I shook my head and gave Baucent a comradely slap on the flank. He snorted at me by way of greeting as I squeezed past him and out of the shelter. Outside the world was completely transformed as it had been snowing while we slept. Everywhere was white, the ground, the stones of the shelter, the sky. The one black spot in all this was the outline of the eagle high above my head.

We saddled up and shipped out as fast as we could. There was little sense in waiting for the weather to get any worse. I trusted Baucent to find his way along the path while the snow was set on the ground but not if the wind decided to throw it around. I wondered whether we had gone as far as we could when I saw a flame burning on a high stone outcrop up ahead.

I pointed it out to Gregor, but he shrugged saying he had never come this way before. The flame was a tiny point of light that grew steadily bigger as we travelled onward and gradually, I realised that it sat atop a tower not unlike a castle keep.

'Is it a giant's house?' said Gregor.

'It may be,' said I, 'Let's find out.'

We rode up to a bridge that spanned a deep chasm, the bottom of which was lost in mist. On the other side was a solid wooden gate. Apart from the beacon burning on the rooftop the castle looked like it had been deserted some time ago, there were creepers growing over the stonework and shuttered windows held shut by thick curtains of spiderweb. I patted Baucent and together we crossed the bridge.

I banged on the door with my gloved fist, raising a cloud of dust. Moss grew over the hinges and I wondered when the last time was that this entrance had been used? A spider on the wall ran for cover in a crack in the cement.

'Nobody home,' said Gregor, 'best we turn back. Perhaps visit the sea instead. We could go fishing.'

'Quiet,' I said, 'I can hear something.'

A hatch, no bigger than the palm of my hand, opened in the broad wooden gate, two beady eyes looked us up and down.

'What are you doing here?' Came a voice.

'What is it? Let me look,' said someone else.

'Get off me, I'm talking to them,' said the first voice.

'But I want to see,' said the second.

'In a moment,' said the first voice, 'now, where was I? Oh yes, what do you two want?'

'There are two of them?' said the second voice.

The tiny viewing hatch slammed shut and the sound of a scuffle came to my ears. Something broke with a clatter and then another hatch opened lower down than the first.

'I can see eight legs,' said the second voice, 'does that mean there are four of them?'

I banged on the gate.

'Good day to you,' I said, 'We are Sir Guillaume of Saint Hilaire and Gregor the Great and we come to pay our respects to the lord or lady of this fine castle.'

'Is he talking about us?' said the second voice.

The hatch slammed shut and the sounds of a scuffle resumed, then a clatter and a bang, a creak and a shudder and the gate slowly began to open. Baucent and I retreated as a cloud of dust and an avalanche of moss tumbled down the front of the ancient castle gate. I looked over my shoulder and saw that my companion had retreated to the other side of the bridge.

'Come in esteemed guests,' said the owner of the first voice, as I live and breathe and tell you this tale, the speaker was a rather well dressed cat, a Ghjattu volpe, 'my name is Filippo and my friend here is Giavannuzza.'

This Giavannuzza, I declare was also an animal who would usually go by the name of Reynard in the fields and forests from where I was born. Her foxes tail sprouted from the rear of a fine silken gown and on her feet was a pair of gleaming buckled shoes. Baucent snorted his disapproval and I am afraid I had to agree with him, but I saluted them both and bid them good day as we entered the courtyard of their castle.

'Thank you for receiving us. Are your Lords and masters at home?' I said.

'We are our own Lords and Ladies,' said Giavannuzza, 'and bow to no one, certainly not the King of the Animals.'

'Hush,' said Filippo, 'he has terribly long ears.'

'He's not coming back here,' said Giavannuzza, 'no one ever comes here, we are the only folk that know that here is here.'

'Where is here?' I said.

'Welcome to the Castle of Forgetting,' said Filippo, bowing low, 'this is where everything that has ever been forgotten or lost is collected.'

'Even this castle has been forgotten,' said Giavannuzza.

'Have we been forgotten?' said Gregor.

'I remember you,' I said, 'so no, it does not apply to you, and I am certain that I am remembered by many people, not least my brothers and my parents.'

'But they do not think of you all the time, so you are forgotten for most of the day,' said Filippo.

'You remembered your family for a moment, but you have only just thought of them,' said Giavannuzza.

'My existence does not depend on whether and how often others think of me.' I said, 'It depends on whether I have eaten enough to give me the strength I need to do battle with fiends and other foul creatures. I remember myself well enough to remain thank you.'

'And my poetry will sustain my memory for centuries,' said Gregor.

'That it will,' I said, 'for in truth, your poetry is remarkable.'

The fox's eyes narrowed, and she smiled a faint smile.

'You must stable your mounts and come feast with us in our hall of memories gentlemen,' she said.

'It will be a great honour,' said Filippo, 'to see what you have already forgotten.'

Baucent fussed and whinnied but I reassured him that I would be sleeping in the stables tonight ready for a quick getaway in the morning. Gregor the Great settled his pony in the otherwise empty stables and together we agreed to my plan, that whatever happened at supper we would make our beds here.

The meal that was provided was extraordinary, with every kind of roasted fowl and sauces spiced with aromas from across the known world. There were fruits I did not recognize, and bread made into fabulous shapes.

'I commend your kitchens,' I said to our hosts.

'It is nothing that you have not seen before,' said Filippo.

'Seems it is rather simple fare,' said Gregor the Great.

'I adore eating with our guests,' said Giavannuzza, 'to see what surprises come along.'

'I once had an eel pie that I will never forget,' I said, 'the eels were still alive, swimming in a gravy sauce beneath a thick pie-crust. I could not eat it and so ended up insulting the ogre who had insisted I join him for supper.'

I caught a glint in the fox's eye, which was surely not a portent of good things to come. I peered at a pie on a plate just out of reach and in my imagination, I fear I saw it move a little. In a bid to change the subject and bring the meal to a close I stretched and yawned, covering my mouth with the back of my hand.

In so doing I closed my eyes for what must have been the slightest instant, but when I opened them the entire world had changed, and I was no longer in the grand dining room of that peculiar castle. Instead, I was in the woods close to the manor where I was born, and I was holding a basket half filled with mushrooms. It was just before dawn, the perfect time for mushroom picking with the morning dew still lying soft on their skin.

The full moon was still high in the sky and there, in front of me, was an enormous wolf, as big as a man. It looked at me with huge dark eyes. Its tongue lolled and dripped saliva. In the soft light I could see specks of blood on its teeth and chin. I stayed absolutely still, waiting for it to pounce, but instead it vanished into a thicket of holly. A moment later my older brother, Charles, the priest, was at my shoulder, his rough cassock pulled close about him in the morning chill, a red stain on his beard.

The sound of applause pulled me back into the dining hall. Giavannuzza the fox and Filippo the cat were clapping and banging the table.

'Very good,' said Filippo.

'Now you remember what made you go off mushrooms,' said Giavannuzza.

'My brother,' I said.

'Loup Garou,' said Filippo.

'No, Charles is a priest,' I said.

'He is both,' said Giavannuzza.

'Never mind that,' I said, 'it is but sorcery and I will not stand for it. Come Gregor, we are leaving.'

'But eel pie,' said Gregor, 'I love eel pie.'

'You can have as much as you want when we get back to the port,' I said.

'To the port?' said Gregor.

'Yes,' I said, 'you are coming with me.'

'You are free to leave of course,' said Filippo.

'If you can remember the way,' said Giavannuzza.

I looked about the room but there were no windows or doors anywhere to be seen. Gregor jumped up and ran about banging on the stone walls with his tiny fists.

'Stop it Gregor,' I said, 'There is a better way. Recite some of your poetry.'

'My poetry?' said Gregor.

'I may never ask you again as long as I live,' I said, 'so make sure you remember your best poem.'

Gregor the Great, hermit and poet of the Corsican mountains, drew himself up to his full height and began to recite a love poem, or perhaps it was a battle hymn, it was hard to tell. I watched as the amused faces of our hosts turned from smug to horrified as the true awfulness of my tiny friend's art manifested itself in that haunted place. I pushed my thumbs into my ears for my protection and cheered him on.

After just a few stanzas the room regained its doors and windows. Minutes later the roof vanished revealing the star-filled sky. The walls crumbled, the table laid with its rich food faded away and the fine tiled floor was replaced with loose mountain scree. I spied Baucent and the pony tied to a scrub oak.

'What are you waiting for?' said Baucent.

I picked up Gregor and dropped him on his steed, mounted Baucent and, with a roar we were away. Behind us a cat and a fox squatted in the dirt, the cat licking his paws, the fox switching her tail. Together Gregor and I galloped away down the mountain to where we could see the full moon reflected in the sea.

'I never knew you could talk Baucent,' I said to my horse. He whinnied in return. I never heard him speak again.

Gregor and I did not ease up our rushing ride until the moon set and the sun rose, and we arrived in a small fishing village with a white sandy curved beach. The fisherman's brightly painted boats were drawn up in a row and the smell of grilled sardines met our nostrils. The food at the castle must have been an illusion for I never felt as hungry as I did that morning. We stopped and ate at a seafront shack, fish with bread made from chestnut flour, and a hot strong brown drink made from local herbs.

We were told the road back to Bonifacio was not long but to watch out for the mustachio'd bandits we might encounter along the way, for they were fierce and always on the lookout for travellers to rob. They were something of a scourge on the fishing village who preferred a simple life of fishing, fetes and singing competitions, and had grown tired of raids and robberies. To be honest with you my friends I was pleased to hear this as I was itching to knock some heads together after the trouble of the last few days.

Baucent decided when it was time to make camp, tired out as he was from all the travelling we had done. We made a fire on the beach and settled to watch the stars come out and the moon return, but I was restless and so asked Gregor to recite some more of his poetry. He was happy to oblige. I put my fingers in my ears and waited. Sure enough, his words had attracted some attention.

'For goodness sake shut the devil up!' came a shout from within the forest, 'or we will shut him up for you.'

Gregor continued to recite for another few minutes but stopped when five mustachio'd bandits appeared at the top of the beach, swords drawn.

'That's better,' said one.

'Now give us all of your money,' said another.

'And your horse,' said a third.

'And the pony,' said the fourth.

'Or what?' I said.

'Or you die, and we take them anyway,' said the fifth and biggest mustachio'd bandit.

To be honest I do not remember much about the next fifteen minutes except that the itch I had been dying to scratch was satisfied very well. I tied the bandits together with their own ropes and helped myself to one or two of their provisions. I am not a monster, when they came around from being knocked out, I did allow them some of their own rum, after which we all spent quite a merry evening around the campfire. They were particularly pleased to hear about the castle in the mountains behind the fishing village which was guarded by just a cat and a fox.

In the morning I let the bandits go and Gregor and I made haste for Bonifacio. When we arrived, the ship was almost ready to sail, and I am happy to say that I was able to visit Rome as planned and that I also travelled all the way to Palestine and back. Gregor the Great proved to be a fine companion and I do believe he has since worked very hard and put the entire enterprise into rhyming couplets, which, one day, we might all avoid listening to.

# Gufi the Fool

Poor Gufi was a fool. There's no nice way to say it. His mother Lucia despaired of him. But she was a shrewd woman and knew how to take care of things. Christmas was coming and she knew that Gufi had to work to make some money.

She sent Gufi to her cousin the innkeeper. He would put Gufi to work in the tavern. It would keep him out of her hair. But after just one hour the innkeeper was close to despair and so he gave Gufi a wine barrel to take to the beach to clean out.

'And don't come back until it is as clean as can be!' said the innkeeper.

So Gufi, who was a happy and good fool, worked hard on the beach, cleaning and scraping the barrel. He worked all morning until the thought came to him, 'How will I know when this barrel is clean enough? Who can I ask?'

There was not a soul on the beach, but a little way off was a fishing boat, which had just put out from the harbour. Gufi waved and called until he had their attention. Fearing some calamity ashore the Captain turned back at once. When they were close enough the Captain called out, 'What is the emergency?'

'Thank you, sir,' said Gufi, 'but I need to know whether my wine barrel is clean enough.'

At that the Captain was enraged. He shouted and called poor Gufi any number of names which I fear I am unable to recount as I am not a qualified sailor. The Captain waved his arms and conjured so strenuously that his face became quite red.

'But what should I have said sir?' asked Gufi.

The Captain drew in a deep breath, regained his composure after a minute or two and said, 'Say Lord let them go faster, so we may make up the time you have lost us.'

So Gufi thanked the Captain for his wisdom, picked up the wine barrel and returned to the path from the beach to the town, calling out as he went, 'Lord let them go faster! Lord let them go faster!'

On his way he came across a hunter taking aim at some plump wild rabbits.

'Lord let them go faster! Lord let them go faster!' said Gufi, and the rabbits pricked up their ears and dashed away before a shot could be fired.

'Why you little so-and-so,' said the hunter, 'why would anyone go and do that? I should turn my sights on your backside!'

'Please sir,' said Gufi, 'I really am very sorry. What should I have said?'

'Say Lord let them be killed,' said the hunter, 'then my family might enjoy a good rabbit stew for supper.'

So Gufi continued on the path into town with the wine barrel on his shoulder, thinking of the hunter and his supper, and calling out, 'Lord let them be killed! Lord let them be killed!'

Almost at once he met two men in a violent argument, their fists raised ready for a fight.

'Lord let them be killed! Lord let them be killed!' said Gufi, and the men at once turned on him.

'What?' said one man, 'You would fan the flames?'

'What is it to you?' said the other, 'You would have us fight to the death for your own amusement?'

And so the two set into Gufi, their own disagreement forgotten.

'Please sirs,' said Gufi, 'I really am very sorry. What should I have said?'

'Say Lord let them be separated,' said one man, while the other nodded in earnest agreement, now his brother in all things.

So Gufi continued on his way, calling out as he went, 'Lord let them be separated! Lord let them be separated!'

As it would happen, he found himself passing the church,

from which a joyful crowd was emerging, with the Bride and Groom at their head as Husband and Wife.

'Lord let them be separated! Lord let them be separated!' said Gufi at the top of his voice.

The Husband was furious and flew into a rage, his new Wife was mad as well. 'What? Are you thinking to put a curse on our first day of wedded bliss?' she said.

'I should thrash you and tan your hide!' said the Husband.

'Please I am so sorry!' said Gufi, 'I don't know what I should say!'

Seeing he was a fool and that there was no malice in him the couple at once smiled, because there was little that could dampen their true joy. 'Say Lord make them laugh,' said the Bride.

So Gufi put down his barrel and climbed on top so to mimic the priest in his pulpit, 'Lord make them laugh! Lord make them laugh!' he said as loudly as he could, and so the young couple laughed, because the fool was a very funny sight indeed.

Soon Gufi was back on the path back to the inn with the barrel on his shoulder, calling out 'Lord make them laugh! Lord make them laugh!' as he went, and people he met all seemed to find his command irresistible.

But then he came upon a crowd all dressed in black, gathered at the door of a house where all the shutters were drawn tightly closed and a single candle could be seen fluttering in the hallway.

'Lord make them laugh! Lord make them laugh!' said Gufi.

'How dare you?' called out one of the mourners, 'How can you say such a thing at such a sad time?'

Gufi set down the barrel, tired of trying to say the right thing. No matter how hard he had tried, all day he had upset people. 'I don't know what to say anymore.' He sat down on the barrel and put his chin in his hands.

'Just say nothing, nothing at all,' agreed the mourners.

Gufi thanked them and the mourners wished him well as he left them and at last, he arrived back at the tavern.

'So, what have you been doing all day?' asked the Innkeeper.

'Nothing, nothing at all,' said Gufi.

'Nothing?' said the Innkeeper, outraged.

'Nothing, nothing at all,' said Gufi.

'So, what should I pay you,' asked the Innkeeper, 'for doing all this nothing?'

'Nothing, nothing at all,' said Gufi.

'Right enough,' said the Innkeeper, 'Now get out of my sight and don't come back tomorrow.'

Gufi went home tired and penniless to his Mother.

'What did you do today son?' said his Mother.

'Nothing, nothing at all,' said Gufi.

'And what did my good friend the Innkeeper pay you?' said his Mother.

'Nothing, nothing at all,' said Gufi.

'So, what do you think we will be having for supper?'

'Nothing, nothing at all,' said Gufi.

His Mother looked about their tiny cottage. In the corner was a trunk. She opened it with an old rusty key and drew out a skein of fine silk.

'Here, take this in to town and sell it so we may eat.'

It was a very fine piece of cloth and was sure to fetch a good sum, but his Mother Lucia was worried that a buyer might talk Gufi into accepting too low a price, so she said, 'Whatever you do you must not sell this cloth to a chatterbox!'

So Gufi picked up the roll of silk and walked back into town. The first person to show interest in the cloth heaped praise upon the colour and the weave.

'I can't sell this silk to you,' said Gufi, 'you talk too much!'

The next person to show an interest went on at length about the exquisite quality of the stitching.

'I can't sell this silk to you,' said Gufi, 'you may never stop talking!'

Then Gufi came to a small square in the centre of which stood a plaster statue.

'Good afternoon,' said Gufi, 'would you like to buy this fine silk?'

He waited a moment and then said again, 'Do you want to buy my cloth?'

A minute later, when he again had no answer Gufi said, 'At last, a person of few words. I would be happy to sell you this silk.'

He hung the cloth over the out-stretched arm of the statue and said, 'I will return in an hour for my money. Is that agreed?'

A minute of silence later Gufi said 'Good. Then it is agreed. I will return in an hour and meet you back here.'

Gufi returned home and as soon as his Mother saw him without the cloth, she asked him for the money.

'I will return for the money in a little while. Everything has been agreed,' he said.

'But is this person trustworthy?' said his Mother.

'You know how you hate a chatterbox Mother, well this man said not a single word. In the market square I could hardly hear myself think for all the hot air from people wanting to buy the silk.' Said Gufi.

At the appointed time Gufi arrived back at the square to collect the money. The statue was there waiting, but the silk had vanished.

'So, you liked it well enough then?' said Gufi, 'So now you can pay me.'

The statue didn't answer.

'What did you like the most? Was it the fine stitching?' said Gufi.

The statue didn't answer.

'Don't tease,' said Gufi, 'I expect it was the fine pattern?' The statue didn't answer.

'So now you can pay me,' said Gufi, 'If you don't want a conversation that is okay. Just pay up and I will be on my way.'

Gufi waited but no bag of coins was produced, there was no jingle of gold or silver, no move made.

'What are you waiting for?' said Gufi, 'Pay me or I'll show you a thing or two.'

Gufi raised his fists at the statue. 'Come on and pay me or you'll be sorry,' he said.

At last he picked up a garden broom and struck the statue across the back of its legs. The plaster statue shattered into a thousand pieces and clattered down across the square. At the base of the statue was revealed a pot brimming with gold. Quickly Gufi gathered it up and ran home to his Mother.

'Mother!' he said, 'He did not want to pay me, so I hit him with a broom and then he gave me all this.'

As we have learned already, Gufi's Mother Lucia was a shrewd woman, and so she took and hid the money straightaway.

# Notes on the Text

Mandorlinfiore: (Literal trans.) Almond Blossom. The original folk tale, which seeded this story, was germinated in the region of Abruzzo on the Adriatic coast of Italy. It can be found in translation in many collections. I first came across it in Italo Calvino's amazing collection of folk stories, which I have been reading and re-reading for more than twenty years. There are other versions, but all are steeped in the lore that your destiny is inescapable. I recast the story on the island of Corsica.

Belfioré: (Literal trans.) Beautiful Blossom. This was the name used for the Princess in the Calvino version of the tale. Her role has been expanded within this telling in order to invest her with more agency.

Baba de Camelo: (Literal trans.) Camel's Dribble. A very sweet and simple to make Portuguese caramel pudding: Modern Recipe: take a can of sweetened condensed milk, place it in a bain-marie for 90 minutes in order to make dulce-de-leche. Separate 5 egg yolks and whisk in the dulce-de-leche and leave to cool. Whip up the egg whites until they are firm, then add to the egg and dulce-de-leche mix and gently fold together until combined. Pour the final mix into a serving bowl, or individual ramekins as required and refrigerate for a few hours until they firm up. Serve with a sprinkling of almonds. Alternatively pop the pud into the oven for 15 minutes at 390F to turn it into a caramel soufflé. Enjoy!

Corsica: The most fabulous island in the Mediterranean Sea. Visit if you can, but beware, there be dragons…

Mazerre: A traditional supernatural role that a Corsican may be called to in their sleep, sometimes unwillingly. Some have turned to the Church to rid them of the 'calling'. A Mazerre lives a parallel night-time life in their

185

sleep, hunting animals which, if caught and killed, turn into people, known to the Mazerre, and usually from the same village. It is said that whoever the Mazerre has hunted and killed will be dead, in the real world, within a year. There are stories of Mazerres doing battle in the dream world with rival gangs of Mazerre. This dream world is very like the actual world, but, according to reports, it is usually swathed in strange mists.

LUomo di Cagna: (The 'Old Man of Cagna') A mountainous outcrop of granite which dominates the skyline to the West of Figari.

Filitosa: A Prehistoric landscape of standing stones to the South Western tip of Corsica. These stones are especially unusual for the markings carved upon them. They consist of either an 'evil eye' design, or a human face. There is a long traditional fear of the 'evil eye' in Corsica, which can be given, and cured, only by a select few practitioners of the dark arts.

Mustachio'd Bandits: What more can I say about mustachio'd bandits that you don't already know by now? Although the Italians among you might call them 'Brigantaggio' while the French may use the word 'Scélérat'.

King of Zonza: Zonza is a mountain town in Southern Corsica. It had a Royal visitor in the person of King Theodore of Corsica in 1736. Theodore was a German adventurer, the son of a Westphalian nobleman who convinced Corsican rebels that he could liberate the island of Corsica from Genoese rule. He had some moderate success but squabbling among the rebels (mustachio'd bandits to a man) led to their downfall. King Theodore died in London in 1756.

In more recent times Mohammed V, Sultan of Morocco, lived at Zonza for five months in 1953 following a coup d'etat. The cold weather eventually led the Sultan to relocate to the Ile Rousse. In 1956 Mohammed V was able to return as Sultan to Morocco.

King of the Animals: This character appears in any number of Italian folk tales. He embodies the trickster who dazzles with a glamour supported by a usually bloody, hidden truth. The King of the Animals will lure you to his fabulous home where you will be attended by invisible servants, chefs and musicians, not realizing that it will be your fate to join them, unless you can discover the game and escape.

Solenzara: So named for the river that reaches its end by the town.

Bonifacio: Today's City was founded as a fortified outpost under the rule of the Barons of Tuscany in 828AD but has been a site of habitation from pre-Roman times. It was named for Boniface the 2nd of Tuscany. He had beaten back the Saracens to North Africa and took the harbour for a naval base. Il Torrione, a round tower, still remains from these times.

These days there are tour-boats and super-yachts to be found in the harbour. In the city there are hotels and restaurants with food you wouldn't believe, just make sure that, before you order, the waiter is not invisible.

Gufi the Fool: Gufi is known in Italian as Giufa and is the overwhelmingly good-natured fool who will always come good, no matter what the odds are. He usually helps to convey a moral or code of behaviour, and it is the actions of those with whom he interacts that are judged as wanting, rather than his own outrageous antics. He is the star of many Sicilian Italian folk tales, and may be one of the etymological roots of the terms to goof, to be goofy, goofiness etc. Giufa's own roots are said to be from the Turkish Islamic tradition of Nasruddin, which came to the island of Sicily when it was under Islamic rule (965-1091AD).

Giavannuzza: is a Sicilian nickname for the fox, a 'puss-in-boots' character who is unusually generous in most tales and is not appreciated, thus precipitating a less than providential outcome for the protagonist.

Baucent: The name of Guillaume d'Orange's horse, the famous knight who campaigned under Charlemagne and supported his successor, the weak and rather foolish King Louis (as he is depicted in the poems). The knight, most likely the Duc de Toulouse from the 8th Century, fought the Saracens in Spain and never ran from a fight, famously goading some brigands and beating them with the hind leg of a horse which God then heals!

Ghjattu volpe: This is the Corsican descriptor for a species of wild cat, also known as 'cat-foxes' which, while it might be related to the African forest cat and possibly the European wild cat researchers believe its origins are Middle Eastern. Shepherd's tales tell of goats and sheep being attacked by the cat with the fat 'fox-like' ringed tail and ferocious teeth. Obviously, nothing like our cultured friend Hector.

# Acknowledgements

No book ever happens in a vacuum, no matter what authors might tell you, or creative writing gurus preach regarding the lonely obsessive trade in words, sitting for hours in a cold back room, conjuring up word pictures and imaginary friends. No. This book in particular was wrought over several years in any number of kitchens, accompanying hundreds of meals and untold cups of tea. At one point we even found ourselves building the head of Rosa-Fury on a sandy beach in Cornwall, such was the level of engagement.

I have to thank Megan, Maya and Jemima for their patience and re-reading skills, pointing out continuity and character issues where they arose and helping to maintain my focus as the story grew.

I also have to thank Maya for her dragon and Jemima for her mustachio'd bandits, and Tom for telling me he wouldn't want to read an unfinished book, so I had better get on and finish it.

All of the photography and image manipulation is mine (with help from Jemima) and has appeared on the blog as illustrations for excerpts, apart from the photograph of the treasure, which I purchased from an online library as I have been unable, so far, to discover any secret troves hidden away by mustachio'd bandits.
I am still looking…

# Author's Note

I have had a lifelong interest in folk tales. These are among the oldest stories that we tell ourselves, either round a fireplace or in the tavern. In Sussex, where I grew up, there were numerous stories featuring pixies, the devil and dragons who lived at the bottom of cold dark ponds. It was said that the devil had a particular fear of Sussex as cooks in that county could make a pie out of anything.

I moved to Somerset with my family and discovered yet more dragons lurking in the Severn and in the hills behind Glastonbury.

Today we live in the Loire in France close by a secret valley where there is said to be a fountain of youth, discovered by an ancient King. There are ghosts and dragons too, so we are always on our guard...just in case.

The formal bit…

Simon Kellow Bingham studied Medieval Literature at Middlesex and Bristol Universities in the UK. He lives with his family in North Western France.

He has also published a narrative poem, The Stonecutter's Tale, set in Medieval London.

You can read more and follow Simon for news of future projects at https://14thcenturypoet.wordpress.com

CPSIA information can be obtained
at www.ICGtesting.com
Printed in the USA
LVHW092321060921
697120LV00014B/841